Alain Mabanckou was born in 1966 in Congo. He currently lives in LA, where he teaches literature at UCLA. He received the Subsaharan African Literature Prize for *Blue-White-Red*, and the Prix Renaudot for *Memoirs of a Porcupine*.

Praise for *Broken Glass*

'*Broken Glass* is a comic romp that releas<u> </u> humour... Although its cultural and intertextual musings could fuel innumerable doctorates, the real meat of *Broken Glass* is its comic brio, and Mabanckou's jokes work the whole spectrum of humour' Tibor Fischer, *Guardian*

'Broken Glass proves to be an obsessive, slyly playful raconteur... the prose runs wild to weave endless sentences, their rhythm and pace attuned to the narrator's rhetorical extravagances... With his sourly comic recollections, Broken Glass makes a fine companion' *Independent*

'A dizzying combination of erudition, bawdy humour and linguistic effervescence' *Financial Times*

'An incredibly funny novel, often rueful, on the edge of tragedy and imbued with the spirit of the French classics. There's a tremendous spirit, irreverence and humour in this book' Boyd Tonkin, Chair of the Judges for the Independent Foreign Fiction Prize 2010

MEMOIRS
OF A
PORCUPINE

· ·

ALAIN MABANCKOU

Translated by Helen Stevenson

Soft Skull Press
AN IMPRINT OF COUNTERPOINT | BERKELEY

Library of Congress Cataloging-in-Publication Data is available.

ISBN: 978-1-59376-436-4

Cover design by Kimberly Glyder
Interior design by Folio at Neuadd Bwll, Llanwrtyd Wells

Soft Skull Press
An imprint of Counterpoint
1919 Fifth Street
Berkeley, CA 94710

www.softskull.com

Distributed by Publishers Group West

10 9 8 7 6 5 4 3 2 1

This book is dedicated to my friend and protector, the Stubborn Snail, to the customers of *Credit Gone West* and to my mother, Pauline Kengué, who handed down this story (give or take a few lies)

how disaster brought me
to your feet

so I'm just an animal, just a *dumb, wild animal,* men would say, though if you ask me most of them are dumber and wilder than any animal, but to them I'm just a porcupine, and since they only believe in what they can see, they'd see nothing special in me, just one of those mammals with long sharp quills, slower than a hound dog, too lazy to stray from the patch where he feeds

I wouldn't want to be a man, to be honest, they can keep their so-called intelligence, for years I was the *double* of a man they called Kibandi, who died two days ago, most of the time I stayed hidden just outside the village, and went to him late at night, for specific missions, I know if he'd heard me making this confession while he was alive he'd have punished me severely, free speech, he'd have said, ingratitude more like, he may not have shown it, but all his life he felt I owed him, I was just a lowly bit player, a pawn in his hands, well, I don't want to boast, but I could say the same about him, without me he'd have been a bit of rotten pulp, his life as a man worth less than a few drops of piss, the piss of the aged porcupine who ruled over us back when I still belonged to the animal world

I'm forty-two years old now, I still feel very young, and if I was a porcupine like the ones that hang about in the fields near the village I would never have lived this long, because for porcupines round here gestation lasts between ninety-three and ninety-four days, at best we live to twenty-one in captivity, but who'd want to spend their life cooped up like a slave, imagining a life of freedom beyond barbed wire, I'm sure some lazy animals wouldn't mind, and might even grow to forget that the sweetness of honey does not soothe the bee sting, I prefer the ups and downs of life in the bush to those cages where some of my comrades are kept, only to end up one day as meatballs in some human being's pot, it's true I have had the good fortune to beat the survival record for porcupines, to live the same number of years as my master, I won't say it was exactly a sinecure, being his double, it was hard work, it made great demands on my senses, I carried out my orders to the letter, even though towards the end I began to step back a bit, thinking maybe we were digging our own graves, but I had to obey him, I was stuck with my role as a double, as a turtle is stuck with his shell, I was my master's third eye, his third nostril, his third ear, which means that whatever he didn't see, or smell, or hear, I transmitted to him in dreams, and if ever he didn't reply to my messages, I'd appear before him just as the people of Séképembé were going out into the fields

I wasn't present at Kibandi's birth, not like some doubles, peaceful doubles they're called, who are born the same day as the child, and watch them grow, their masters never see them, they intervene only when necessary, when their initiate falls ill, for example, or has a jinx put on them, it's a dull life, being a peaceful double, in fact I don't know how they stand it, they're soft and slow, the slightest noise sends them running, a foolish way to behave, starting at their own shadow, I've heard it said that most of them are deaf as well as blind, but you can never catch them out, they have a perfect sense of smell, so they protect their human, guide him, follow his every move until his dying day, when they, too, lie down and die, and their power is transmitted by the grandfather at birth, the old man seizes the babe after consulting the progenitors, disappears round the back of the hut with it, talks to it, spits on it, licks, shakes and tickles it, tosses it in the air, catches it again, and while this is happening, the spirit of the peaceful double leaves the body of the old man and enters that of the little creature, the initiate dedicates himself to good works, will be noted for his boundless generosity, will give money to the lame, the blind, the poor, will respect his fellow man, study plants to heal the sick and be sure to pass on his gifts to the next generation the day his first grey hair appears, it's a very dull life, a monotonous life, you might say, I'd have no tale to tell you if I'd been a peaceful double, with no particular history, nothing out of the ordinary to speak of

no, I'm one of the *harmful doubles*, we're the liveliest, scariest kind of double, the least common, too, the transmission of this kind of double, as you can imagine, is more complicated, more tightly regulated, it occurs in the child's tenth year, he has to be made to take the initiatory drink known as *mayamvumbi*, an initiate will drink it on a regular basis, to achieve the drunken state in which he produces a body double, his *second self*, a bulimic clone, who, when he's not snoring away in the initiate's hut, spends his whole time running, cavorting, leaping over rivers, burrowing about in leaves, and there I was, caught between the two, though not just as an onlooker, without my intervention my master's other self would have succumbed to the ill effects of his gluttony, because I'll tell you this, the parents of a child who receives a peaceful double will know all about the initiation and encourage it, but the transmission of a harmful double takes place against the child's wishes, without the knowledge of mother, brothers or sisters, the humans of whom we become the animal incarnation will cease to feel emotions like pity, understanding, empathy, remorse, compassion, night will enter their souls, once transmission has occurred, the harmful double must leave the animal world and come to live close to the initiate, performing his assignments without protest, when did you ever hear a harmful double contradict the master on whom his existence depends, tell me that, never in living memory of the porcupine, that's when, and elephants aren't the only ones with perfect memories, that's just another human prejudice long before my master started playing with fire, while I was enjoying a few months' pleasant rest, just watching life unfold around me, fresh air in my lungs, a skip in my step, I ran, how I ran, and at the top of a hill I would pause, and look down at the bustling wildlife all around, I liked watching other animals, the rhythm of their daily lives, I was getting back to the bush, at times I just disappeared, with no word to my master, I'd watch the sun go down, and close my eyes and listen to the crickets, and wake next morning to the chirrup of cicadas, and during these periods of inactivity, or respite, I was constantly feeding, the more I ate, the hungrier I got, I can't remember now how many tuber fields I destroyed, bringing great distress to the peasants of Séképembé, who put the blame on a half-man half-animal, with a stomach as deep as the pit of their own ignorance, then at dawn I'd go down to watch the ducks bobbing about on the river, the reflection of their gaudy plumage shimmering on the swell, how funny they looked, gliding not drowning, then one of them one would give the signal for the end of play, or the approach of a hunter, and off they'd fly, up and away, then some time towards noon came the procession of zebras, followed by the female deer, then the wild boar, then the lions, roaming in groups along the river, the little ones at the front, the old ones roaring at the slightest thing, they never overlapped, they seemed to share out the day between them, and only much later, when the sun was already high in the sky, came the army of monkeys, I'd see the males fighting, usually over a question of precedence, or a female, it was quite amusing really, their gestures reminded me of humans, especially the anthropoids, poking their bogeys, scratching their genitals, then sniffing their fingers and expressing disgust, and I did wonder whether some of them might not be harmful doubles to humans, then I told myself to get a grip, I knew harmful doubles had to stay well away from communal life

yes, I was a happy porcupine back then, I'm putting up my quills as I say this, that's our way of swearing a pledge, another is to raise the front right paw and wave it three times, I know humans swear on the heads of their ancestors, or in the name of the God they've never seen, the one they worship with their eyes tight shut, they spend their whole lives reading His word in a big book which was brought here by white men in the days when the people of this country hid their absurd little organs under leopard skins or banana leaves, unaware that over the horizon there lived other people, not like them, that the world stretched on, far beyond the seas and oceans, that when night fell here, elsewhere the sun still shone, and as it happened, my master, Kibandi, owned this book of God, with all the stories men have forced themselves to believe, on pain of not deserving a place in what they call *Paradise*, you won't be surprised to hear I had a look at it myself, out of curiosity, since, like my master, I was a good reader, sometimes I would read for him, when he was tired, I had a good look at the God book, whole pages at a time, some thrilling, some touching, I underlined some passages with my quills, I'd already heard some of the stories with my own little ears, from the lips of some pretty respectable people, with little grey beards, who attended the village church on Sundays, told with such precision, with such great faith, you could only think they must have seen these things with their own eyes, I should add that the bit of the story they tell most often, these bipeds, is the one about this mysterious guy, a kind of wandering charismatic, the son of God, they'll tell you, how he came to be here was all very complicated, there's nothing about how exactly his parents mated, he's the same guy that walked on water, and turned water into wine, and multiplied the loaves to feed the crowd, and gave respect to the prostitutes, when everyone else threw stones, and made the lame to walk, even the hopeless cases, and the blind to see, and he came down to earth to save the whole of humanity, including us animals, because, get this, even back then they wanted to preserve at least one sample of every living species, we didn't get forgotten, they put us all into this cage called *Noah's Ark*, so we'd survive a torrential rainfall, for forty days and forty nights, *the deluge*, it was called, but then many centuries later God's only Son was sent down to earth, men didn't believe him, they persecuted him, the bad people whipped him, crucified him, left him out in the blazing sun, and the day of his trial, at the hands of the very same people who accused him of causing a public nuisance with his spectacular miracles, they had to choose between him and another man, a wretch they called Barabbas who feared neither God nor man, they chose to set the brigand free and kill the other one, the poor son of God, but believe it or not , he came back from the dead, like someone just waking up after a quick siesta, and the reason I'm going on about this mysterious guy is not to get away from the subject of my confessions, but because I'm quite sure this guy, the son of God, really was something special, an initiate, like my master, but he must have been protected by a peaceful double, he never hurt anyone, it was others went looking for lice in his tonsure, well anyway, Kibandi had stopped reading those stories, and moved on to more esoteric things, probably because he thought the book of God would condemn his beliefs and practices, and seek to divert him from teachings of his ancestors, so my master didn't believe in God at all, particularly since God always put off answering his prayers till tomorrow, when he wanted concrete results today, to hell with the promise of paradise, that's why sometimes he cut short the hard core believers in the village, saying something like 'if you want to give God a good laugh, just tell him your plans', and it's all very well men swearing on the heads of their dear departed, or by the name of the Almighty, which they've done since the dawn of time, they never keep their word, in the end, because they know very well that a word means nothing, you only have to keep it if you believe back in the forest after a mission, I'd go and think things over for a while in a burrow, at the top of a tree, in a hollow trunk, or even by the river's edge, far from the parade of ducks, the procession of animals, I'd review what we'd been doing, me and my master, while he slept long and deep, recovering his strength after an exhausting night, I might think and think till the evening of the following day, it never tired me, in fact I enjoyed grappling with the abstract world, and I learned early on to discriminate, to look for the best solution to a problem, I don't know why men think themselves so superior, I'm sure they're not born intelligent, they may have a certain aptitude for it, intelligence is a seed which must be watered if is to flourish, and grow into a well-rooted fruit tree, some people will always be ignorant and uncultivated as a flock of sheep, following one of their number over the edge into a ravine, others will always be fools, like a certain astrologer, a poor cretin who fell down a well, or the old crow who snatched a sheep because he saw an eagle do it, and others will cling to their stupidity, like the agama, that excitable lizard who tosses his head from dawn till dusk, such humans will always live in the twilight zone, their sole consolation being their humanity, the aged porcupine who used to govern us would have snapped 'they're all cretins, their bottom line is we're humans, but a fly's not a bird, just because it can fly', what I'm saying is that while I sat there thinking, I was trying to understand what lay behind each idea, each concept, I know now that thought is of the essence, it's thought that gives rise to human grief, pity, remorse, even wickedness or goodness, and while my master brushed these feelings aside with a wave of his hand, I felt them after every mission, many's the time my face was wet with tears, because, for porcupine's sake, at times of great sadness or compassion, you get a lump somewhere right near your heart, your thoughts turn black, you regret your actions, the bad things you've done, but as I was only carrying out orders, devoting my life to my role as a double, I managed to get a grip on my black thoughts, and tell myself, by way of comfort, that that there were worse things you could do in this life, I'd take a good deep breath, gnaw at a few manioc roots or palm nuts, try to get some sleep, tell myself tomorrow would be another day, and soon I'd be given a new mission, and I'd have to prepare myself, leave my hiding place, make my way to my master's house or workshop, receive his instructions, of course, I was free to rebel, I did sometimes dream of escaping my master's clutches, it sometimes crossed my mind, the temptation was strong, there were certain acts I could perhaps have avoided, but it was like a kind of paralysis, and I didn't act, even yesterday, when the only option was the cowardly one, to flee like a peaceful double, as my master breathed his last and passed on to the next world, I waited and watched while he endured his final death throes, a scene which stays etched in my mind, pardon my emotion, the tremor in my voice, I'll just pause here, take a few deep breaths by rights I should have left this world by now, I should have died the day before yesterday, along with Kibandi, there was total panic, total shock, we were caught short, we had no contingency plan for an event of this kind, I turned back into a wretched little scarpering porcupine, in fact at first I didn't realise I was going to survive myself, and since a double normally dies the same day as his master, I thought I must be just a ghost, and when I saw Kibandi gasping his last, surrendering his mortal soul, I was immediately thrown into a panic, because, as our old governor used to say, 'when the ears are cut off, it's time for the neck to worry', and I didn't know what to do, where to go, I was running round in circles, space seemed to be shrinking around me, I felt like the sky was about to fall in, I couldn't get my breath, everything was terrifying, I told myself I needed immediate proof of my existence, but what proof is there ever that one exists, that one is not just an empty shell, a shadow without a soul, well, I had picked up a few handy tricks from the men round here, I just had to ask myself what the difference was between a living being and a ghost, first I told myself that I thought, therefore I must exist, now I've always said that men don't have the monopoly on thought, anyway, the inhabitants of Séképembé, in any case, say that ghosts can think too, since they come back to haunt the living, and have no problem finding the paths which lead to the village, they wander around the markets, go and look round where they used to live, announcing their death in the villages all around, sit down at a roadside bar, order a glass of palm wine, drink like old soaks, settle the debts they ran up while they were alive, and yet as far as the eye is concerned, they don't exist, so one couldn't be sure of anything, I needed a different sort of proof, so I tried an old trick, I waited till the sun rose on Saturday, that was yesterday, and I came out of my hiding place, I looked left, looked right, sat down in the middle of a sort of empty space, waved my front paws, crossed them, uncrossed them, and seeing that, praise be to porcupines, who'd have believed it, my shadow moved, and its movements corresponded to those of my limbs, I was alive, no doubt about it, and I could have just stopped there, you would have thought, but no, I wasn't sure, I didn't want to do anything dumb, I wanted still further proof – the surest kind – that I was alive, so I went to look at myself in the river, and again I waved my front paws around, and crossed, then uncrossed them, I saw my reflection mirror my movements, so I couldn't be a ghost, because what I've gathered so far, what I've picked up from the humans in Séképembé, is ghosts don't have reflections, they lose all physical presence, become immaterial, but I still wasn't convinced of my existence, despite all these irrefutable items of proof, which would have been quite enough for your average villager, I had to do one more test, a more physical one this time, so since by now I was walking along by the water's edge, I dropped down and scrabbled in the dust, took a running jump then flung myself into the water, I felt its chill, and then I knew, this time for certain, that I was still alive, the worst thing is, I would have drowned if I hadn't quickly got out of the water, and straight after that I went back to my master's house, to see how things were developing over there, I hid behind the workshop, and was amazed to see the body of Kibandi, lying under a cover of palm leaves, he had departed this world, for sure, but what shocked me most was that, from a distance, it looked as though his corpse had an animal head, a head looking something like mine, but ten times bigger than mine, or maybe it was the fear of my own demise that conjured up this illusion, it was death, that was clear, death lay here before me, with a heartbeat like my own, ready to pounce on me, maybe in a minute, maybe in an hour, several questions occurred to me, for example 'what if a hunter set upon me', or 'what if there was a flood and I was swept into the turbulent river Niari?', with questions like that going round in my head I just couldn't stay calm, I felt nervous, anxious, at the slightest noise I dashed for cover, like a coward, like a peaceful double, and I went and hid myself in a lair, the first time I'd set foot in it, I was right to be frightened too, because straightaway I heard a reptile hissing, no time to work out what species it was, out I came, rolled up in a ball, terror in my gut, and I said to myself a reptile that hissed like that must be deadly poisonous, I came hurtling out of the lair, I had to cross the main road to get to the houses at the edge of the village, and that was dangerous too, it was a road used by transport trucks once a week, I couldn't remember which day they came roaring like mad things though our region, I decided I wouldn't cross the road, you never know, and I just wandered around where I was, unable to shake off the image of my master with my head on him, I lost a few quills along the way, and then I began to feel ashamed of myself, I was letting my human side get the better of my animal nature, you scumbag you, I said to myself, coward, selfish bastard, I told myself I couldn't just run away like this, and yet I didn't see what else I could do at this point in the proceedings, if I wasn't careful I'd attract the attention of the Batéké dogs and then the whole village would come running after me, to kill me, there was a little voice I couldn't resist, though, that spoke to me, chided me, called on me to show some dignity, to make some gesture which would have pleased my late master, so I went back to Kibandi's hut a bit later, despite the danger of being picked upon by those tailed vigilantes, the Batéké dogs, fortunately they were off duty then, I just had time to make out what was going on in my master's yard, they were preparing to take him to the cemetery, he didn't qualify for the kind of village funeral that lasts at least five or six days, he'd be buried within twenty-four hours of his death, I saw a small group of men carrying the body to the graveyard, I recognised the Moundjoula family, who had been the cause of my master's death, their two children, the twins, Koty and Koté, it was more of a formality than a proper burial, I swear, no one was crying, for porcupine's sake, I wouldn't have been surprised to find the villagers murmuring 'all bad deeds on earth are punished, at last the wicked Kibandi is dead, let him burn in hell', my heart ached to see the way they dragged his coffin along the ground, I'm quite sure the only reason they went through the motions of giving him a final send off was because, even though they may not feel like it, humans will bury even the wickedest man, and the witch doctor gave a funeral oration even though he didn't want to, two guys hurriedly moved to fill in the grave, the cortege left in silence, while I stayed there, staring at the cross they'd cobbled together from two branches of a mango tree, it leaned a bit to the left, stuck on top of a mound of earth which was now my master's tomb, I could make out an old storm lantern that the villagers had left by the tomb so the deceased would be able to find his way in the deep darkness of the next world, and more to the point, so he would never show up again amongst the inhabitants of the villagers, worming his way into the belly of a pregnant woman, what's more, the villagers are convinced that if the dead don't have a storm lantern by their tomb they may go walking over the bodies of the other dead souls, to whom they should show respect because they died before them, which seemed quite considerate of them, considering Kibandi had given them nothing but grief, I saw the group coming back towards the village in single file, I heard their whispers, their conjectures as to the cause of my master's death, I blocked my ears because they were saying things I could scarcely believe, in fact what I wanted was to get closer to Kibandi's last resting place, sniff the earth where he lay, but I didn't, I left, weeping bitterly, angry with myself for fleeing like a coward, I turned round to take one last look at his tomb, then finally left, but with no thought where I might go, night fell upon the village, shadows loomed before me, I could see nothing, by chance I found a place to spend the night, between two large stones, I'd had to scratch way at the earth for quite a while to make a place for myself, I knew it would only be a temporary shelter, I wasn't going to hang around there forever because it's the place where some of the villagers sharpen their hoes before going out in to the fields, and during the night I fought off the desire to sleep because my feeling was that the night and death go together, always have, and when I did actually nod off for a bit, forgetting for a moment that I was under sentence of death, forgetting the image of the corpse with my own head grafted onto it, I dreamed that I was falling into a great hole in the ground, and I also dreamed that I was surrounded by flames, which swept through the bush, throwing even our eternal enemies, the lions, the leopards, the spotted hyenas, the jackals, the cheetahs, the tigers and the panthers, into a panic, I woke with a start, astonished to hear my quills rustling, surprised I could still see things, 'I'm still alive, I'm still alive, I'm not dead, for porcupine's sake', I said to myself, but I had to get out of there fast, so that's what I did only a few hours ago, at the first light of dawn, I mean, today, Sunday, I shook the dust off my belly and my butt, at first I hadn't understood why no villagers had passed by the two large stones where I'd hidden for the night, then later it dawned on me that today is a day of rest, otherwise I would have seen hunters, palm wine tappers and other workers who go out into the fields at crack of dawn, and so, before leaving the stones, I stretched, I yawned, followed my instinct, I shuffled along awkwardly, I don't quite know how I found my way down to the river, where for once the wild ducks and other animals were nowhere to be seen, I wanted to make my way to the bit where the water's less deep, then decided against it, for fear of drowning, then I came across you, which is why, my dear Baobab, I've been sitting at your feet since this morning, talking to you, talking still, even though I'm sure you won't answer, and yet the spoken word, it seems to me, delivers us from the fear of death, and if it could also help me stave it off for a little while, or escape it, that would make me the happiest porcupine in all the world

the fact is, though I'm ashamed to say this, I don't want to disappear, I'm not sure there is life after death, and even if there is, I don't want to know about it, I don't want to dream of a better life, the aged porcupine who ruled over us was right when he declared, enjoying the immediate impact of his thoughts on the group, 'the toad wished so hard for a better lot, he found himself without a tail for all eternity' and in fact the toad didn't just find himself without a tail, he was also afflicted with such ugliness that it would be a crime even to feel sorry for him, and so, my dear Baobab, when men talk of the life to come they're kidding themselves, poor things, in the next life, they think, there'll be a clear blue sky, and angels everywhere, with everything lovely, they'll be in a garden, in the bush, but a bush where the lion has no fangs, no claws, and will laugh, not roar, and no such thing as death, jealousy, hatred or envy, all humans will be equal, well I'll go along with all that, but how can I be sure I'll stay a porcupine, what if I'm reincarnated as an earthworm, or a ladybird, a scorpion, jelly fish, palm tree caterpillar, slug or some other wretched creature of far lowlier status than my present one, a status which would be the envy of any other animal, now you may think I'm just a braggart, a smooth talker, an idiot with bristles, it's not that I go round criticising other species for the mere pleasure of exaggerating, no, it's that modesty can be a handicap, it can ruin your life, that's why, ever since I realised that if you're going to accept yourself as you are it's best to play down your shortcomings, for example, I'd rather have a nice set of bristles than the chronic mange you see on the dogs of this village, there are some wretched creatures in this world I won't even mention, there are always some worse off than yourself, the list is endless, it would be quicker to count my tens of thousands of quills than to list every animal with a grudge against the world's creator, I'm thinking of the poor old tortoise and its rough shell, the elephant with its awkward trunk, the hapless buffalo with its ridiculous horns, the filthy pig, stuffing its snout in the mud, the snake, condemned to slither about on its belly, the male chimpanzee, with his testicles that hang down like gourds of palm wine, let's not even mention the duck, with its squishy webbed feet, like a gastropod's, there are so many pitiful creatures here below, my own species are by no means the worst off, and if human beings were a bit more truthful themselves, they'd agree with me, because, for porcupine's sake, if you'll just excuse me for upping the tone a moment, I wasn't one to be content with nibbling away at the bark a few metres from where I slept, idling my time away down a hole, gnawing the bones of dead animals or the fruit which had fallen from the tree, and once my mission was accomplished, let me tell you, I'd go back into the forest, and huddle up alone, though I'd never minded solitude until last Friday, I pondered the meaning of my relationship with my master, but let it not be thought that I was at such times overwhelmed, devastated, caught in the trap of my master's curious destiny, oh no, I want to live in the here and now, I want to live just as long as you do, and between you and me, I'm not going to decide I've no right to live, and take my own life, let's be quite clear about that, I'm trying to look on the bright side, I'd still like to have a laugh now and then, to show laughter's not just for humans, for porcupine's sake

I don't know if you noticed a remarkable thing this morning, when I began talking to you, I didn't want to draw your attention to the fact, but I noticed a rather elderly lizard coming towards me, he stopped a few metres away, looked behind him, put out his tongue, waved his tail, I saw his eyes staring in amazement, as though he'd been turned into a statue of salt, terrified at the sight of me chatting away to myself, he took a risk and darted off down a rat hole, I laughed like a hyena, because I hadn't had a good laugh like that for a long time, but I quickly put a lid on it because there are people in our village who've died of laughing, and when I think of that poor lizard I wonder if perhaps it was the first time he'd ever come across an animal acting like a human being, speaking coherently, nodding in approval, waving one of his paws in the air to swear an oath, I felt quite sorry for the poor reptile, even though our governor had often said that when I was small I was scared stiff of lizards, the one this morning must have thought he was dreaming, I just went on talking to you, as though it was all quite normal.

it wasn't by chance I came to hide beneath you, I decided the moment I saw you, while making my way along the river's edge, I thought, I'll go and shelter there, the fact is, I want the benefit of your ancestral experience, just from the folds around your trunk it's clear you must have had to learn to live with the changing seasons, even your roots spread wide and deep in the belly of the earth, and every now and then you move your branches to change the direction of the wind, and remind all nature that a long life like yours comes from keeping silent, and here I am, for porcupine's sake, chattering away, startled by the slightest leaf that flutters from your crown, just let me take a few breaths before I carry on, I'm panting a little, ideas rush and crowd my mind, I think since this morning I've been talking too fast, I'd like to drink a little water, I'll just take a few sips of the dew around me on the grass, I'm not going to risk wandering away from you, believe me

how I left the animal world

how long ago it seems, that time when I left my own habitat, and drew close to the boy child I knew affectionately as 'little Kibandi', it's been many years since then, but memories remain, as clear as if it was yesterday, at that time Kibandi and his parents lived in the north of the country, far from here, in Mossaka, a wet region, with giant trees, crocodiles, and turtles as big as mountains, the time had come for me to leave the animal world, and embark on my existence as a double, I had to reveal myself to my young master, and little Kibandi *sensed* I was there, from the moment I started to make him feel my presence, trying to throw a little light on his existence, I don't know what would have happened if we hadn't bonded almost immediately, I came at just the right moment, he was ten years old, the required age for receiving a harmful double, and when I arrived at the gates of his village in the North, I saw the little pup, standing behind his father, like his shadow, I felt sorry for the child, he'd just had his initiation, he couldn't control the drunkenness brought on by the *mayamvumbi*, his father had just put him through a great test, a new world lay before him, he had become a new creature, the fragile thing the villagers of Mossaka could see behind Papa Kibandi was only a puppet now, a kind of hollow container, the contents of which had evaporated, he was just biding his time, till he met his double, when the two would merge and become one, he couldn't sleep, poor little Kibandi, he was so busy struggling with the effects of the ritual drink, and all this time I was getting more and more frantic out there in the in the forest, the bush pressed in upon me, I couldn't bear to be there, I was trying to get out, so I could go and live near my young master's village, at that time I didn't know I would incur the wrath of the old porcupine who used to rule over us, who did nothing but rail against humans, from sunrise to sunset

this was the most turbulent time of my life, when I had to weigh up the demands of the child and our little family of porcupines, I put up with the governor's rages, as he became increasingly intransigent, as though he had got wind of the huge changes taking place in my life, as though he'd guessed what was going to happen to me, he held more and more meetings, sneering down at us, raising his voice, with affected gestures, stroking his little beard with his claws, then crossing his front paws, his snout pointed skywards, in imitation of some human being calling on Nzambi Ya Mpunga, no point our saying anything, he always had the last word, for example, he'd tell us such and such a river used to flow round the other way and when we asked the old guy how long it had taken for the water to make this spectacular change in direction, he'd toss his worn out quills, make a show of closing his eyes and thinking, point to the sky, it made me roar with laughter, and then he got angry and began to threaten us, issuing an ultimatum we all knew by heart, 'if that's how it is, then that's the last time I'll tell you anything about men and their ways, you're just plain ignorant', and when we went on laughing he'd add enigmatically, 'when the wise man points to the moon, the fool looks at his finger', but when he saw I was still keen to go check out what the monkeys' cousins were up to, the aged porcupine flew into a rage, telling his stooges to keep a close paw on me, could he possibly have known I was due to enter upon the scene, now young Kibandi had drunk his initiatory drink, he'd no idea, my dear Baobab, when I left I did it discreetly, sometimes with the connivance of two or three sidekicks, who wanted to hear from me how it really was with humans, because the aged porcupine always tended to exaggerate, and almost seemed to be calling for a war between the animal and human species, I would vanish into the bush for whole days and nights and it got so that that I only felt at ease when I was close to my future master's village, whenever I got back home I found the governor in a rage, calling me every name under the sun, and to further tarnish my image, he'd tell my sidekicks that too much contact with humans had sent me mad, I was heading straight for the fox's jaws, soon I'd have forgotten our ways, I would lose touch with what made us the most noble animals in the bush, he swore, our aged philosopher, that one day I'd get caught in one of those traps men leave in the bush, or worse still, even fall into the silly traps set by the kids from Mossaka, who knew how to capture birds with one of their mother's aluminium bowls, and the other porcupines all laughed themselves silly, because they too considered it better to fall into a trap set by a real hunter than one left by a human being who wasn't yet weaned from its mother's breast, you'd always see them at the gates of the village in the North, but I must say, dear Baobab, that only the birds of Mossaka got caught that way, and mostly the sparrows, who are the stupidest birds round here, I wouldn't like to generalize and say all vertebrates with feathers, beaks and anterior limbs used for flight are that stupid, oh no, I'm sure there are some intelligent species of bird, but the sparrows of Mossaka had such a low IQ that I actually felt sorry for them, sparrows the whole world over must be the same, I can see they must be cut off from the reality of life on earth, constantly flitting here and there, that's who the children of the North had laid their traps for, the little humans, in the middle of nowhere, had these bowls, propped up with a piece of wood, and round them they tied a long piece of string you could hardly see, and they hid in the undergrowth about a hundred metres off, and, drawn by the seed left round the bowls, the poor things jostled and chirruped up in the tree tops then would suddenly all drop to earth at once, without setting up some lookouts to tell them if something was up, then the kids would tug the string of their silly traps and the sparrows would suddenly find themselves imprisoned under the container, but what was strange, dear Baobab, was that none of them had any sense of the danger, which would have been obvious to any animal, even the ones with no common sense at all, it didn't occur to the birds for a moment that it was a bit strange to find a container sitting in the middle of nowhere, that seeds lying on the ground, untouched by other birds, might be a bit suspicious, I never got caught out myself, otherwise I wouldn't be here talking to you now, and so my fellow porcupines, indoctrinated by the governor, were convinced I would get caught in one of these traps, 'the drum is made from the skin of the fawn that strays from its mother', our Australopithecus was wont to say, thinking I wouldn't understand what he meant, and this remark created a great stir within in the group, some of my colleagues repeated it everywhere they went, imitating the patriarch's gestures, teasing me, even, calling me 'the fawn', until one day I got so irritated by their jokes, which did not seem in the least bit funny to me, I explained that the fawn was the young of a wild animal, a deer, a buck or roe, whereas I was in fact a porcupine, and proud of it too once it becomes the harmful double of a human being, an animal has to leave its natural milieu, its family, so my separation from the members of our group occurred down in Mossaka, but considering that porcupines are reputed to be solitary animals, we were fortunate to live in a community, and every evening the old governor held a meeting, made a few general remarks, I could tell he was covertly talking about me, saying no one was irreplaceable in the forest, that he'd known a few jumped up porcupines in his time, he knew how to put them back in their place, and when I didn't react, he became more pointed, muttering things about 'the fish that proudly dallies in the feeder stream one day ends up salted on a slab in the market', he hastened to remind us that I was an orphan, without him I wouldn't have been a live porcupine at all, he said my procreators were as stubborn as me, that they left this earth shortly after my arrival, I was scarcely three weeks old, our governor boasted of how he had taken me in, along with his female mate, now deceased, and he went into how I used to defecate the whole day long, I was a lazy good for nothing, scared of baby lizards, and the others all laughed loudly, and it was from him I learned about the ways of my parents, it seemed they liked to mingle with the human race, they'd disappear by night and go wandering among the humans in Mossaka, returning at dawn the following day, tired out, with red eyes, muddy paws, and spend the whole day sleeping like dormice, the governor couldn't understand it, I had begun to piece their lives together bit by bit, I no longer doubted it, they were harmful doubles, I reached this conclusion the day I felt the call of young Kibandi myself, I accepted the idea that I was descended from a line of porcupines whose destiny was to serve humans beings, not for better, but for worse, for the very worst, and each time I heard the governor talking about the death of my parents it made me angry, he claimed to have tried to spy on them one night, to find to where they went in such a hurry, but they'd given him the slip between two clumps of trees because the old guy already had trouble with his eyes, even back then, a week went by, they heard nothing, then came the dark day, the eighth day since their disappearance, the fateful day when an owl with an injured claw, crushed in a man-made trap, flew over our patch, come, so it seemed, to announce to the governor the sad news already on the lips of most of the animals in our region, he told him that a hunter had killed my parents not far from Mossaka, the whole herd had to move on in a hurry, and find a new patch, a few kilometres away

even so, I ignored what had happened to my parents, since I'd never known them, I let the old governor say what he wanted to the others, I went with my own instincts, and vanished from the bush more and more often, I left no gaps between trips now, and for the first time I disappeared for four days and nights running, I just kept on going straight, it was an overpowering urge, and my comrades started panicking, they looked everywhere for me, they searched the groves round where we often drank, while one of us watched out for hunters lying in ambush round about, but I wasn't there, and finally, in desperation, they made enquiries of the other members of our kind, but they couldn't think of any porcupine that matched their description, some said that when I moved I had a way of sniffing every square centimetre of ground, others added that I usually hid behind trees as though always on the look out for danger, and on that day the governor specified that I moved like a porcupine whose paw has been crushed in a trap of the kind laid by a little chap still sucking his mother's breast, according to him I limped, I hobbled, and several of my comrades shouted him down, as this was a whopping great lie, and they went on looking, because they were fond of me, and as I had always liked to burrow into the hollow of trees, especially trees like you, they first went to look inside baobab trunks, then inside the palm trees nearby, and in so doing invaded the privacy of some squirrels who were quick to chuck palm nuts at their heads, followed by a string of insults in their own tongue, and meanwhile, I was somewhere near Mossaka, trying to absorb the child whose double I was going to become, I had a vague idea of what he was like because he'd appear to me in dreams at dead of night, and from somewhere would come this vibration inside of me, only known to animals predisposed to fuse with a human being, I wanted to be sure not to get the wrong kid, I didn't imagine for a moment I'd be hanging around indefinitely in Mossaka, that I'd be leaving my comrades for ever in fact, dear Baobab, when I left our territory I had not intended to leave for ever, I swear I liked communal life, I was convinced that I could lead a double life, one at night, and the other by day, that I could both stay close to my master and continue to hang out with my comrades, which turned out, alas, to be incompatible with the reality of being a double, and it was when I made the trip to Mossaka that I first felt the influence of the liquid Kibandi had just been made to drink, and I began to vomit, my head started swimming, my vision blurred, my quills grew heavy, I could only keep my eyes fixed straight ahead, rather as though the child was calling for my help, he needed me, I ought to be there, or something dire might happen to him, his life was in my paws, when I breathed I was breathing for him, I was him, and he was me, I had to get to him as fast as possible or something dreadful would happen, my heart was fit to burst, I'd forgotten who I was, where I was, and why I was going to Mossaka, I just had to move forward, walk, advance, follow the path before me, I had kilometres and kilometres to go, of course I couldn't get there that day, but I needed to make a start, and as it was raining that day, once I got halfway there I was obliged to shelter for the night in a cave, till the next day, I should say that I don't like rain much, a number of my fellows have been swept away into the Niari waterfalls and drowned, and inside I found nothing but toads and small mice, whom I was able to intimidate, I got to the outskirts of Mossaka the next day at sunset, and when I finally reached the gates of the village, exhausted, dribbling at the mouth, barely able to keep my eyes open, I went to sleep at the back of a house not far from a river which I had not seen till now, it was a branch of the Niari which cuts the region in two, and there I rested, thinking I would take my time staking out the Kibandi house the next morning, because by night there'd be the risk of hunters or Batéké dogs, and in the middle of the night I felt a strong draught of air, dead leaves were rising upwards, then a strange noise as though something was coming towards me, 'for porcupine's sake, it's a man, it's a man, he's seen me and he's going to kill me, I must flee', I said to myself, panicking suddenly, I was determined to leave my hiding place as quickly as possible, and save my skin, but alas I was paralysed, I couldn't move any of my feet, as though I'd been put to sleep, I was wrong in fact, it was the noise of an *animal* moving about, so I put up my quills without first identifying the animal, which was coming closer and closer, I hoped he'd be stupider than me, that he'd be scared of quills, I was ready to throw them if necessary because unlike most of my kind I know how to, but I didn't have to go that far, the cake wasn't worth the candle, I took a deep breath, and was reassured when I finally saw the animal before me, I almost burst out laughing, almost proved the governor right when he said that during the first few months of my life I would panic even if I saw a baby lizard, there was no need to freak out that day, it was just a lousy rat that looked as though he'd taken a wrong turning and found himself face to face with me, I took pity on him, maybe he wanted directions, I couldn't help him, I didn't know the place myself, and then I thought better of it, the rat seemed pretty strange, he moved at a slug's pace, a sign of age, perhaps, which had robbed him of the use of his back legs, this was not a rat like other rats, he was there for a reason, perhaps to kill me, stop me getting to the Kibandi child, he was challenging me now, with his protruding eyes, he drew back his lips, I stayed still as marble, so he would see I was not frightened of a mere rat from Mossaka, that I'd seen far scarier ones than him in my time, and he circled round me, sniffed my sex, licked it, then vanished through a hole in a shack about a hundred metres away, and I finally realised that this was the shack I was looking for, the old rat was the harmful double of Papa Kibandi, he had come to make sure of my status as double to his son, this was the end of the transmission process which had started with the absorption of the initiatory drink, and that's how transmission takes place, first between the humans, from initiator to initiate, with the absorption of the *mayamvumbi*, then between the animals, the animal double of the initiator must lick the sex of the animal double of his young initiate, in fact the double of Papa Kibandi had wanted to make sure that the animal who would live with his son was courageous, an animal who could keep his cool when faced with danger, if I'd had shown the slightest sign of panic, if I'd tried to make a run for it he'd have wiped me out, not a moment's hesitation, and things had turned out well for him, dear Baobab

it was now four days and four nights since I left the bush for Mossaka, and the news spread among the animals in our neck of the woods, then a rumour went round about a dead porcupine under a palm tree, my colleagues rushed to find it, returning several times to the body, which had been half eaten by red ants, but they decided this porcupine didn't look anything like me, it had a something wrong with its face, they gave up trying to convince themselves, they weren't going to spend their entire lives looking for me, they must just face the facts and accept them, they trooped off into the bush, in single file, I could see the governor already informing my peers of my death, telling them I must have been caught in the traps set by the kids of Mossaka, he'd probably told them I was stubborn by nature, proud, like humans, talked too much, brought down by my own arrogance, preferring life as a tame animal to the freedom of the bush, I imagined him launching into the usual sermon, no doubt giving me a good kick when I was down, like the idiot creature in the story, known to humans as the 'ass', it was a tale he loved to tell, a tale intended as food for thought, *The Town Mouse and the Country Mouse*, he probably told them how one day the Town Mouse invited the Country Mouse for a meal, and the two of them were busy eating in the house of some humans when they heard the master of the house returning, whereupon they swiftly scarpered and when the noise stopped and the danger seemed to have passed, the town mouse suggested to his country cousin that they go back and finish their meal, but the country mouse declined, and reminded the town mouse that in the bush, no one would interrupt you while you were having your bite to eat, and then, dear Baobab, I expect our aged governor would have probably have summed up the moral of this story in one withering phrase, since the majority of my peers would have failed yet once more to grasp it, despite my numerous attempts to explain it to them quietly while the old chap was summing up, with a detached air, 'away with feasts, however great, that may be spoiled by fear', adding in a murmur, no doubt, 'fine food's worth zilch', thereby proving once and for all that a fate such as mine might befall any animal tempted to stray into the world of men, 'thus ended the life of a foolhardy creature, I saw him enter this world a mewling babe, I took him in when he was orphaned, even then he was scared to death of lizards, shitting everywhere, a little guy who never counted for anything, since nature decreed we'd be stuck with these quills, men made drums from deerskins, now let that be a lesson to you', he probably concluded, and I expect it was a sad day for my fellow creatures, but the aged porcupine didn't let that stop him, because in his voluble way, he liked to illustrate his remarks with at least two or three fables, stories his grandparents had told him, I expect he would have referred to my comrades' favourite tale, *The Swallow and the Little Birds*, it seems there was once a Swallow who had travelled far and wide and had seen many things, learned and remembered many things, to the point where she could even warn the sailors of a coming storm, and the Swallow in question, who was knowledgeable and experienced in matters of migration, spoke to the little birds one day, warning them to beware the sowing season, the sowing of the seed could mean disaster for them, said the Swallow, they must take care to destroy the seeds, eat them, one by one, or they would be sure to end up in cage, or in a pot, not one of the little birds listened to the wise Swallow, they covered their ears to block out the reasonings of their feathered friend, who, in their opinion, had spent too much time wandering around the world aimlessly, and lost all judgement, and when her prediction came to pass, much to the surprise of the little birds, several of them were captured, and made slaves, and I expect at this point the governor would have wound up his story, saying, 'we only believe evil when it is upon us', and no doubt he ventured several other allegories while he was on the subject, which, in my absence, went undeciphered, since, as I said before, I was always the one who tried to reveal to the others the hidden sense of the aged porcupine's parables and symbols, and when he'd finished showing off his wisdom with his telling of *The Swallow and the Little Birds*, he'd announce, with the solemn air he liked to affect, 'I am that Swallow, and you are the little heedless birds, these, my words of wisdom and you my uncomprehending listeners', and if my fellows were still puzzled, our aged friend would have treated them to an even more withering remark along the lines of 'none of you understands all this, when the cricket ejaculates, only the old sage hears,' but this time he probably said, in a more serious tone of voice, 'and now let's talk of other things, no one in the bush is irreplaceable, he was a deer calf who acted like a human, it's his own funeral'

as you see, my disappearance caused a lot of grief, especially among those who liked to listen to my tales about humans while the old man's back was turned, pretending to enter a state of deep meditation, he'd bid us leave him to his patriarchal contemplations, go up to the top of a tree, close his eyes, stumble through his prayers, it really was like listening to the genuine first cousin of the monkey, the groaning and mutterings of the porcupine are remarkably similar to human utterance, but to this day, I'm proud to say, I'm pretty sure some of my fellows never gave up hope that one day they'd see me again, I was too careful to get myself captured by the kids of Mossaka like some naive booby, they must have remembered I'd warned them a thousand times about the little traps we liked to sneer at, they admired my lucidity, flair, intelligence, speed, cunning, they knew I could outwit them with one flick of the paw, so it could be my fellows had already begun to imagine the day I'd come back, a great day, they'd laugh in the face of the governor, tell him his sermonising was pure eyewash, ask a thousand questions about my disappearance, my incursion into the world of the first cousins of the monkeys, let's be honest, the first question they asked would have been about the human condition, about how men relate to animals, my fellows had always wondered whether the first cousins of the monkey believed we were capable of thought, of conceiving an idea, pursuing it logically, always wondered if men were conscious of the harm they do to animals, if they realise how arrogant they are, with their self-proclaimed superiority, many of them, in fact, knew nothing of humans beyond the prejudices spouted by the governor, they'd never set paws in a village, they only saw men from a distance, they laughed at the thought of these poor creatures who only used their lower limbs to get from a to b, using only their feet for walking, just to show other species how superior they are, my fellows listened with interest to the caricature presented by our governor, Man he declared, was indefensible, deserved no absolution, was the wickedest of all creatures on earth, attenuating circumstances there were none, and since humans give us animals such a hard time, since they are hostile and deaf to our calls for peaceful co-existence, since they are the ones who come into the bush to hunt us, since they only grasp the need for harmony once they've been decimated by a long battle which is indelibly printed on their memory, well then, we should do likewise, and strike out at their children, even the newborn, because 'the tiger's young are born with ready claws', so spoke our governor, and you see, my dear Baobab, that he had no sympathy for humankind

my death quickly became an accepted fact in our little community, I presume it was the governor who decided that the group must relocate without further delay because, dear Baobab, when one of our number died, we'd set off at once, on a two or three day journey, in search of a new homeland, there were two reasons for this painful migration, first it was thought that a change of place was the only way of shaking off our fears and anxieties, which lay largely in our terror of the hereafter, in the fact that we believed that the next world was populated entirely by terrifying creatures, the governor turned this to his advantage by telling us that when a porcupine dies he revisits his former fellows again a few days later in the guise of an evil spirit, but this time giant-sized, with his quills raised, longer and sharper than the hunters' javelins, and, again, in his version, the quills of such a porcupine scraped against the clouds, darkened the horizon, stopped the day from breaking, so we lived in fear of this phantom coming back from the kingdom of the dead to terrify us, stop us sleeping, pull out our pretty quills, threaten us with its long poisonous spikes, but the second reason for emigrating after the death of one of our number had more to do with survival instinct, we were convinced that a man who had slain an animal in one place would be tempted to return, 'forewarned is forearmed', the governor would say, if he felt that the fear of the phantom of an ill-willed porcupine was insufficient to persuade us of the necessity to move on, and if he saw we still weren't happy with his decision, despite his threatening talk, he would say mysteriously, 'trust me, I'm like a deaf man running till he's out of breath', adding, 'and if you do see a deaf man running, my dears, don't ask questions, follow him, because he hasn't heard the danger, he's seen it', and this is possibly why my fellow porcupines had left the place where we'd been living for some time, leaving no clue as to how I might find their new territory, and even if some of them had thought of guiding me towards it by whatever means, by, for example, leaving palm nuts along a path, or quills on the ground, strewing excrement, or spraying urine as they went, marking the trunks of trees with their claws as they passed, it wouldn't have helped, the governor would have destroyed the signs, he probably posted himself at the rear so as to keep a watch on the migration and above all, to destroy any such clues

and so it was that on the fifth day, when I returned to our territory to rest after my first contact with young Kibandi, I found no one from our group, all was calm, the burrows were deserted, and I realised at last that the governor must have given the order to clear out and I had been declared dead by my own people, faced with this emptiness, I started to sob, the slightest noise in the undergrowth revived my hope that I might find one of my fellows coming to embrace me, rubbing his quills against mine by way of joyful greeting, teasing me, calling me 'little fawn', and when at last I did hear something, my quills began to tremble for joy, alas, my enthusiasm was short lived, and I realised that it was only a palm rat venturing forth, his sinister laughter said it all, even now I don't understand why these lovers of palm nuts hate us so much, obviously I did not respond to his challenge, his silly snickering, I stayed there alone for six days, on the seventh day I noticed a squirrel of a fairly advanced age hanging about, and since at least squirrels are rather friendlier towards us, and we've never actually come to blows with them, I asked if he'd seen a bunch of porcupines leaving the region a few days before, he burst out laughing too, and did all the things we most dislike about his species, dashing about wildly for no reason, rolling his eyes, twitching his nose, bobbing his head about in an epileptic fashion, all of which looks quite ridiculous, but having said that, these tics are often what saves them from the humans' rifle, and I noticed that his tail, which dragged behind him, was damaged, perhaps he had narrowly escaped a human trap, the wound was still gaping, I had no wish to dwell on the origin of his misfortune, then, after sniggering, and performing a series of absurd tics, he scratched his behind and mumbled, 'I've been spying on you, I wondered why you were crying like that, it's because you're looking for the others isn't, it, well I can't say I've seen any porcupines round here for a few days, it's been rather quiet round here just lately, it's as if there's nothing more left to eat, so everyone's gone, but anyway, if you've got nowhere to live, you can come and join us, if you like, I'd be delighted to introduce you to my fellows, particularly since the rainy season's coming up and it looks like it's going to be a really tough one, judging by the heavy clouds hanging low as an ass's belly, come with me, we should help each other out, lend one another a paw, know what I mean', I couldn't see myself living with squirrels, putting up with their tics, sharing their nuts, intervening when they fell out over a rotten almond, climbing trees all day, so I shook my head, he tried to persuade me, I didn't waver, I'd rather die than stoop that low, I said to myself, and he went 'who d'you think you are, eh, pride won't find a vagabond shelter when he's wandering about in the rain', and I replied, 'a vagabond's shelter is his dignity', and that silenced him, he looked me up and down and then said 'listen, my spiky friend, I offered you hospitality, you've refused it, I'd like to help you find your friends but I'm in a hurry just now, the others have been waiting for me all this time, they sent me out to find some nuts, but I can at least tell you your family went the other way, behind you,' and he pointed with his snout towards the horizon, where the earth meets the sky, where the mountains merge like a little heap of stones, I knew he was teasing, that it gave him a thrill to see me in such a state, 'I'm sorry, I have to be off, good luck, be brave, and let's hope your dignity finds you a home', he said, and off he went, without turning round, I looked at the horizon, then at the sky, I wiped my tears, I dithered about for a few minutes, emptiness all around, still, as though the silence was looking back at me, watching me, knowing which way my fellows had gone, I could picture them exactly, the governor speaking, praying, muttering orders, I stopped crying there and then, and taking a large gulp of air, my quills at half-mast, I said to myself 'too bad, now I'll live on my own', and after two more days of gnawing loneliness and misery, I set off on the path to the village of my young master

and that, dear Baobab, is how I left the animal world and

joined the service of young Kibandi, who had just received his initiation in Mossaka, the boy I would later follow all the way to Séképembé, the boy I would stick to for decades, up to last Friday, when I could do nothing to save him from death, I'm still feeling sad about it, I'd rather you didn't see my tears, so I'll turn my back to you, out of decency, and rest for a moment, before I carry on

how Papa Kibandi sold us
his destiny

not a day of his life went by without my master thinking of the night his father sold on his destiny to us, visions of the initiation haunted him, he was back in Mossaka, aged ten, it was night, a night full of terrors, of flying bats, when Papa Kibandi woke him without a word to his mother, and dragged him off into the forest, and even before he left the house, little Kibandi witnessed something so incredible, he had to rub his eyes several times, to be sure it really was his father, one lying next to his mother and one standing beside him, so there were two identical Papa Kibandis in the house, one asleep in the bed, the other moving around, and in a sudden panic the child cried out, but his father, the one standing, put his hand over his mouth and said 'you saw nothing, I am me, and the one lying next to your mother is also me, I can be myself and my *other self*, you'll soon understand', little Kibandi tried to escape, the standing-up father easily caught him, 'I can run faster than you, and if you escape, I'll send the other me after you', little Kibandi looked again at the father standing up and the other one lying down, it felt like he was being kidnapped, perhaps he should wake up his father's other self, and he'd come to the rescue, but then he wondered if the lying down one really was his parent, the standing up father let him check, then nodded, to say that he was the one the child had to talk to, he was his father, the real one, little Kibandi was speechless, the standing-up father nodded again, gave an enigmatic smile, my young master cast a last despairing glance at his parents' bed, his mother now had her hand on the lying-down Papa Kibandi's chest, 'my other self won't even wake up till everything's over, in accordance with the ancestors' wishes, and if he does wake up now, you'll find yourself without a father, come on, we have a long walk ahead', he grabbed the child with his right hand, almost roughly, the door was ajar, they vanished into the night, the father always with his hand on the child, as though afraid he might run off, they walked and they walked, the only sound was the cries of the night birds, and when at last they came to the heart of the bush, under the eye of the watchful moon, the father let go of my young master's hand, he knew it was too late to run off now, he was too afraid of the dark, Papa Kibandi brushed aside a tangle of creeper, headed for a field of bamboo, picked up an old spade lying hidden under a pile of dead leaves, the child watched carefully, they turned back, went into a clearing, you could hear a river running somewhere down below, and Papa Kibandi began to sing in his gravelly voice, while digging the earth as skilfully as a *grave digger*, one of those shroud-stealers who, once they've committed their theft, and desecrated the sepulchre of the stiff within, immediately wash the burial cloths in the river, fold them up neatly, and set off to sell them at full price in any neighbouring village where there might be a funeral, Papa Kibandi went on digging, the sound of the spade hitting the earth pierced the silence of the bush, and after about twenty minutes, which was like an eternity for my young master, the father threw down the tool on the pile of earth, heaved a sigh of relief, 'right, that's perfect, we're there now, soon you'll be released', and he lay down on his belly, plunged his hand down into the hole in the ground and drew out an object wrapped in a piece of filthy cloth, and inside the child found a gourd and an aluminium cup, Papa Kibandi shook the gourd several times then poured the *mayamvumbi* into the cup, took a gulp himself, clicked his tongue, then held the vessel out to his son, who shrank back, 'hey it's for your own good, come on, drink', and he grabbed him with his right hand, 'you've got to drink this potion, it's to protect you, don't be stupid', and when little Kibandi began desperately to struggle, he pinned him to the ground, held his nose, forced him to drink the mayamvumbi, a few mouthfuls was enough, it worked straight away, little Kibandi at once began to feel dizzy, fell to the ground, got up, swayed, could hardly stand, his eyes were shut, the liquid tasted like palm wine, but also like swamp mud, the potion burned his throat, and when he opened his eyes, my young master saw a child who looked just like him, he just caught a glimpse of him, before he vanished between two bushes, 'you saw him, your *other self*, didn't you, you saw him', said Papa Kibandi, 'he was there in front of you, it's no illusion, my boy, you're a man now, I'm very happy, you're going to follow the path I received from my father, which he got from his father before him', little Kibandi was staring at the spot where the boy, his other self, had vanished, he could still hear dead leaves being trampled underfoot in his flight, an insane flight, as though someone was chasing after him, and there was silence, at last his father could breathe again, he had waited so long for this moment of liberation, when the duty of transmission would finally be fulfilled little Kibandi didn't have much to do with his other self, who spent most of his time trailing me, stopping me sleeping, I'd hear him walking on dead leaves, running till he was out of breath, or breathing quietly in the bushes, drinking water from a stream, and sometimes I'd find food supplies piled up near my hiding place, I knew little Kibandi's other self had left them there, and it was at such moments, I guess, that I felt comforted, I was glad to be privileged, I put on weight, my quills grew stronger, I saw them gleaming when the sun was at its height, I grew used to the game of hide and seek with my young master's other self, he became a go-between, and when I hadn't seen or heard him for two or three weeks, I felt uneasy, I'd set out in haste for the village, reassured only when at last I saw little Kibandi playing in their yard, I'd return to my hiding place, reassured, and so the years went by, the other self and my young master fed me, I lacked for nothing, I had no care for tomorrow, I only had to stick my snout out of the entrance to my refuge, there were my supplies left waiting for me, and if any other animal dared come and help themselves, my young master's other self threw stones to drive them away, for once I had to agree with what humans say, I had a pretty easy life things were fairly quiet during my master's adolescent years, we learned to get along, to synchronise our thinking, to know one another, I'd send messages to little Kibandi via the other self, then one day I was hanging around in a backwater when I came across him sitting on a stone, he had his back to me, I stopped moving, made no noise, or he'd have run off again, he was watching the herons and the wild ducks, I suddenly felt such a wave of emotion I almost thought it must be the real little Kibandi sitting there with his back to me, I moved forward a few yards, he heard me, at once he turned, too late, I had seen his face, though he looked just like my master, the strangest thing was, Kibandi's other self had no mouth, no nose either, just eyes, ears and a long chin, I stared in amazement and at once he was off into the bushes, leaping into the backwater, and the herons and the wild ducks took flight, hiding him in his confusion, then he was gone, leaving only ripples in the water, it was one of the very few glimpses I would ever get of my young master's other self, the last time was when the creature without a mouth came to tell me that my master and his mother were about to leave for Séképembé, a few days before Papa Kibandi died it was as though with age Papa Kibandi was returning to the animal state, he stopped trimming his nails, when he ate he did it just like a real rat, he scratched his body with his toes, and the people of Mossaka, who had always treated it as a rather sick joke, an old fool's game, began to worry about it, the old man developed long sharp teeth, particularly at the front, tough grey hairs sprouted from his ears and straggled down to his jaw, and whenever Papa Kibandi disappeared around midnight, Mama Kibandi never even realised he'd gone, she just saw her husband's other self lying in the bed by her side, my young master would suddenly find columns of rats marching up and down in the main room of his parents' house, he knew the largest of these rodents, the rat with the big tail, flattened back ears, and hooked paws was his father's double, he mustn't whack him with a stick, though one day, for fun, he'd sprinkled rat poison on a piece of tuber and left it at the entrance to the hole where the rodents came out, a few hours later there were a dozen or so rats lying dead, while his parents slept my young master quickly gathered up the defunct rodents, wrapped them in banana leaves, and went and disposed of them round the back of the hut, but in the early dawn, to his great surprise, Papa Kibandi came and gave him a talking-to, saying 'if you want to do away with me, get a knife and kill me in broad daylight, it's thanks to me you are who you are today, ingratitude is an unforgivable sin, I hope I won't have to speak to you about this again', Mama Kibandi knew nothing more about it, father and son understood each other

and there were so many deaths in Mossaka, one hard upon the other, nose to tail burials, you'd no sooner finished lamenting one dear departed, and there was another one lined up, Papa Kibandi didn't go to the funerals, which got people asking questions in the village, where everyone knew everyone, he saw people looking at him, crossing the street to avoid him, with his rat-like air, and then there were the women who gossiped about him at the river bank, his name came up at every meeting in the palaver hut, children wept and clung to their mothers' skirts as soon as the old man appeared, and even the Batéké dogs barked from a distance, or from their masters' doorways, the whole of Mossaka now had it that there was *something* about Papa Kibandi, every detail of his life was scrutinised, examined with a fine toothed comb, it was strange, they said, how he hadn't had many children, just the one, when his hair had already turned grey, he was prime suspect for any one of these deaths, take his own brother, Marapari, for example, who died sawing down a tree in the bush, when he was the best woodchopper in Mossaka, eh, it's true that the brother had changed his working method, had got himself an electric saw, something you needed to learn to use, in this part of the world where everyone still used axes, perhaps Papa Kibandi was jealous of this piece of equipment, then, envious of his brother's savings, which came from the profits from its use, from hiring it out, and what about the death of his younger sister, Maniongui, who was found limp, lifeless, with wide staring eyes, the day before her wedding, eh, everyone knew Papa Kibandi was opposed to the union for some reason to do with regions, 'no marriage between a northerner and a southerner, and that's that', he'd say, and what about Matoumona, the woman Papa Kibandi wanted to take as his second wife, a woman of half his age, eh, did she not die when her corn soup went down the wrong way, and Mabiala the postman, who seemed to be interested in Mama Kibandi, and Loubanda the tam-tam maker, who was just too successful with women, and Senga the brick maker who wouldn't come and work for him, and Dikamona, who sang at vigils for the dead, who snubbed him, and had publicly called him an old sorcerer, and Loupiala, the first qualified nurse Mossaka produced, a young woman who, according to Papa Kibandi, talked a lot but said nothing, and was always showing off her diploma, hm, and Nkélé, the biggest farmer in the region, a selfish man who'd refused him a plot of land by the river, eh, what had happened to all these people not related to him, who popped off one after the other, ah, my dear Baobab, these disappearances were all blamed on Papa Kibandi, while he gazed serenely into the middle distance, as though there was nothing he could do about any of it, as though he were above what he himself called 'petty disputes of lizards', and since no one would speak to him, he gathered his hurt pride about him and told his son and wife not to speak to the rest of the village, not to say hello, and whenever he passed another villager he spat on the ground, he called the village chief all sorts of names, called him wretched and corrupt, said he only sold land to his own family, and then there was the fateful business of the family conflict which the people of the north were never to forget, the falling out with his sister, the youngest in the family, and she should have known better, because here again, Papa Kibandi would shuffle the cards with his own hand, sow doubt in the minds of the villagers, postpone what should have been the end of his earthly existence, only Papa Kibandi could pull that off, believe me, dear Baobab, and to this day I still can't believe he took them all for such a ride

it was during the dry season in Mossaka, when the waters of the Niari river scarcely covered the bather's ankles, that the terrible event occurred, one day at sunset they found the lifeless body of Niangui-Boussina on the far bank of the river, across the water from the village, her belly swollen, her neck puffed up as though she'd been strangled by a criminal with giant hands, she was none other than the niece of Papa Kibandi, the daughter of his younger sister, Etaleli, whom I will call Aunt Etaleli, as my master did, Ninagui-Boussina was a teenager who had come to spend her holidays in Mossaka with her mother, their village was a few kilometres away, Aunt Etaleli insisted her daughter could not have died from drowning, not that, no way, she was born on the banks of the most dangerous river in the country, the Louloula, she'd spent her childhood in the water, it was an odd business, Papa Kibandi's name obviously came up, Aunt Etaleli said she wasn't leaving Mossaka until some light had been shed on the drowning of her daughter and as tensions began to rise, she left her brother's house and went to stay with a friend, and did not leave her house until the day the body of the young girl was to be brought back to Kiaki, the village where

Aunt Etaleli lived with her husband, and this time Papa Kibandi heard the word 'sorcerer' the minute he set foot outside his house, they called him 'plague rat', wouldn't let him put his case, he would have liked to discuss it with his sister, point out that they could accuse him of many things, but not of *eating* his niece, and when I say *eating*, my dear Baobab, you must understand that I am talking about terminating someone's life by means which are imperceptible to those who deny the existence of a parallel world, in particular incredulous humans, well then, for porcupine's sake, on the day of Niangui-Boussina's burial in Siaki, they waited for Papa Kibandi with poisoned spears, they planned to skewer him in public, in the very village where he was preparing to come to pay his respects to the memory of his niece, at the last moment he changed his mind, the old rat he'd sent ahead to sniff things out caught wind of what was afoot, how Aunt Etaleli, along with some of the other inhabitants of Siaki, had set a trap for him, but anyway, a week after the funeral Aunt Etaleli showed up in Mossaka again early one morning, with a delegation of four men, she shouted at Papa Kibandi, saying openly, 'it was you that ate Niangui-Boussina, you ate her, everyone knows, everyone says so, now look me in the eye and admit it', Papa Kibandi denied the accusation, 'I didn't eat her, how could I eat my own niece, hm, I don't even know how you eat someone, the girl died of drowning, that's all there is to it', and his sister got to the point and said, 'if you've got any balls come with us to Lekana, the witch doctor Tembé-Essouka will pick you out in front of these four witnesses, one of them is from Mossaka anyway', and to everyone's surprise, perhaps also because there was such a crowd pressing in around them, Papa Kibandi offered no resistance, just put on his rubber shoes, pulled on a long boubou, and said defiantly, 'I'm all yours, let's go, you're wasting your time, sister', and Aunt Etaleli replied 'don't call me sister, I'm no sister to an *eater*'

the four witnesses who'd come with Aunt Etaleli had been chosen from four different villages, as tradition required, to ensure that that whatever these people reported back to their different localities would be neutral and faithful to the truth, the little group walked for half a day till they got to Lekana, home of the famous witch doctor Tembé-Essouka, an old man, born blind, with spindly little legs, and a beard which grazed the ground as he moved his head, it seems the local leaders revere his knowledge of the dark arts and go to him for advice, he never washes, for fear of washing away his powers, he wears a tattered old red garment, does his business by the side of his bamboo bed, can control the rain, the wind, the sun, requires payment only on results, and even then you pay in cowrie shells, the currency which was used at the time when this country was still a kingdom, he doesn't trust the national currency, he thinks times haven't changed, the official currency's a delusion, that the world is made of kingdoms, each with its own sorcerer, and that he is the greatest sorcerer of all, and as soon as they reach his house on the hill he gives a great snort of derision, which always terrifies visitors, then he'll start telling you in detail about your past, the exact details of your date and place of birth, the names of your father and mother, tells you why you've come, shakes the terrifying masks hung up above his head, communicating with them, this was the man who would decide between Kibandi's father and his aunt, the four witnesses had tried everything they could to reconcile brother and sister, who had not spoken a single word to each other while they were walking through the bush, the group arrived at the gates of Lekana around midday

dear Baobab, the people of Lekana were used to a flow of people coming to consult Tembé-Essouka, who, on hearing visitors' footsteps, shouted from his tumbledown house, 'hey, you there, what do you think you're doing here, Tembé-Essouka isn't here to sort out trivial matters you could easily settle among yourselves, don't come bothering me for nothing, I don't need your cowries, the guilty man hasn't come with you, I see water, yes, I see water, I see a young girl drowning, she's the niece of an old man being accused by a lady, if you insist, if you don't believe me, enter at your peril,' and since Aunt Etaleli was more determined than ever, the group entered his hut, and it was not so much the putrid smell that repelled them, all six, but the masks, who seemed angered by the strangers' stubbornness, their temerity, Tembé-Essouka had a damp, exhausted look about him, he was sitting on a leopard skin, fiddling with a rosary made from the bones of a boa, whose head was nailed above the entrance to the hut, the visitors sat down on the floor, and the fetichist set to thinking, murmuring, 'disbelievers, I told you the culprit wasn't with you, why have you entered my hut then, do you doubt the word of Tembé-Essouka, or what', Aunt Etaleli got onto her knees, began sobbing at the sorcerer's feet, she wiped her tears on the edge of the pagne knotted about her waist, the sorcerer pushed her away, 'let's be clear about this, this house is not a place for tears, there is a cemetery a bit further down, you'll find any number of carcasses there who'll be happy to receive your tears', but still Aunt Etaleli stammered 'Tembé-Essouka, my daughter's death is not a normal death, people shouldn't die like that, I beg you, look carefully, I'm sure you'll help me, the whole country is in awe of your great knowledge', she began sobbing again, despite the sorcerer's annoyance, 'hell's teeth, silence, I said, do you want me to kick you out of here, d'you want me to send an army of bees to buzz you, eh, what is this business, then, who d'you think I am, do you still not understand, that the old man here, the one you're accusing of this misdeed is not the one who ate your daughter, how many times do I have to tell you, *dammit*, and now if you insist on knowing the truth, I will reveal it to you, because I see everything, I know everything, and to convince you of the innocence of this man you've brought here, you must all undergo the trial of the silver bracelet, too bad, don't say you weren't warned, I'll give you ten seconds to decide whether I begin the trial, yes or no'

you won't believe me, dear Baobab, Papa Kibandi at once accepted to undergo the trial of the silver bracelet, while even those who reckoned they had nothing to worry about were thinking twice about it, firstly because Tembé-Essouka was as blind as a bat, secondly because the outcome of the trial could be affected by panic, Papa Kibandi was not going to back off, Aunt Etaleli had suddenly dried her tears, she seemed to delight in advance in the idea of seeing her brother exposed before four witnesses, the fire lit up the hut, crackling like the fires which tear through the bush in the dry season, the masks seemed to move their thick lips, whispering occult phrases to the sorcerer, to which he responded with sudden shakes of the head, smoke swirled round the visitors' faces, each coughing and spluttering louder than the next, a smell of something rotten, then of charred rubber caught in their throats, and when the smoke finally cleared Tembé-Essouka placed a pot filled with palm oil on the fire, threw in a silver bracelet, let the oil boil for some time before plunging his hand straight in, the boiling oil came up to his elbow, he recovered the bracelet without burning himself, showed it to the astonished group, put it back in the pot, 'now it's your turn, madame, you do the same', after a second's hesitation, Aunt Etaleli plunged her hand into the pot, seized the bracelets, almost cried victory, and the witnesses, reassured, all did the same, again with success, and the sorcerer turned next to Papa Kibandi, 'it's your turn, I've made you go last, because you are the supposed eater', Papa Kibandi immediately obliged, and triumphed, under the watchful eye of Aunt Etaleli, while the other witnesses turned to stare at the accuser in amazement, the sorcerer said, 'the four witnesses and the man unjustly accused will now leave this hut and wait outside, and I will reveal to you, madame, who it was that ate your daughter', Aunt Etaleli stood alone facing the masks, who by now looked disgusted, and the sorcerer was deep in thought, eyes closed, and when he opened them Aunt Etaleli had the feeling he wasn't actually blind at all, he looked her straight in the eye, gave a bark like a Batéké dog, the fire suddenly died, he began counting his beads again, chanting something Aunt Etaleli didn't understand, his eyes rolling, this time lifelessly, his thumb and index finger seized one of the biggest beads, he stroked it nervously, stopped his chanting, took the aunt's right hand, asked her 'now who's this guy they call Nkouyou Matété I see in my thoughts, eh', Aunt Etaleli stared, then gathered her wits to say, 'Nkouyou Matété, you did say Nkouyou Matété', she asked, 'you heard me, who is he then, he's very strong, he's hiding his face, but I can still make out his name, he's surrounded by other men, they seem to be arguing, issuing death threats', and Aunt Etaleli muttered sceptically, 'it can't possibly be him, he's my husband after all, he's the father of my late daughter, you mean to say it's him, well, I mean, it's not possible, he wouldn't eat his own daughter, I tell you, surely', 'it was he who ate the girl , he's in a club that meets in the village of Siaki by night, and every year one of their members sacrifices to the other initiates someone dear to them, this season it was your husband's turn, and since his harmful double is a crocodile, your daughter met her death by water, drawn into the current by her father's animal, now the last word is yours, either I call in the four witnesses and your brother, whom you accuse, or you choose silence and keep what I've told you to yourself', without a moment's hesitation, Aunt Etaleli said 'I want you to do something to my husband, I want you to put a spell on him, I want him to die before I get back to Siaki, he's a bastard, a scoundrel, a sorcerer', Tembé-Essouka almost recovered his sight he was so angry, who do you take me for, eh, I have never put an evil spell on anyone, I simply observe, help those in difficulty, and for anything else, go and talk to the rogues and charlatans in your own village, I am not one of them, who do you take me for, eh', 'please, Tembé-Essouka, at least say nothing to the men waiting outside, I particularly don't want my brother to find out, I accused him wrongly because of the people of Mossaka, they say he has a harmful double who's a rat, so you can see why, surely, put yourself in my position,' the sorcerer stood up, as far as he was concerned the meeting was over, and before showing Aunt Etaleli the door he said, 'that's

your problem, I will say nothing to anyone, Tembé-Essouka has
done his job, don't forget to shut the door behind you and to leave
some cowries for the ancestors in the basket at the entrance'

the group left Lekana, the four witnesses all bombarding Aunt
Etaleli with questions, she stayed silent as a clam, and since she
still seemed angry with Papa Kibandi, who had a big smile of
satisfaction on his face, he went off in the opposite direction, he
walked for two hours and never once turned back, it was only
much later that he expressed his joy, began singing songs, like
a madman, what a comeback, and since his thoughts naturally
strayed to the scene of the silver bracelet which had just proved
his innocence, he burst out laughing, murmured something
a little as though he were thanking someone, headed into the
forest, looked about him, there was no one, not even a bird, and
then he lifted up his long boubou around his waist, squatted
down as if he was about to do his business, breathed out sharply,
held his breath, pushed, pushed, pushed again, farted gently,
a palm nut shot out of his anus, he grabbed it, inspected it,
brought it to his nose, smiled and said 'my dear Tembé-Essouka,
you really are blind', Papa Kibandi had good reason to laugh
at the famous sorcerer, he had just become the first man ever
to have caught out a sorcerer of Tembé-Essouka's stature, but it
was a mistake to cry victory too soon

Tembé-Essouka didn't make mistakes, though, dear Baobab, we
should have known that, and two months later, he turned up
at Mossaka, and the people were sore amazed, fear crept into

their shacks, their animals took cover, the sorcerer had news for us, what could it be, and in any case, he was blind, how had he found his way through the bush, then they said perhaps he was faking blindness, he could see everything, the village headman gave him a distinguished welcome, he admitted that for the first time his knowledge of the dark arts had failed him, he proved that Papa Kibandi was a threat to the entire village, he revealed the old man's tricks, said most of the deaths in Mossaka were his doing, announced that to date Papa Kibandi had eaten more than ninety-nine people, 'I have come here for you, I am here to deliver you from this evil, for this man is the most dangerous man in all this region, let him not eat his hundredth victim', he said, and to back up his claim, he quoted, from memory, in alphabetical order, the names of his ninety-nine victims, only one of them lived outside of Mossaka, young Niangui-Boussina, Tembé-Essouka explained her death, a swap between Papa Kibandi and an initiate in the village of Siaki, none other than the Aunt Etalie's husband, Papa Kibandi had set it all up, he had eaten his own niece, 'I am here today to deliver you from this devil, Papa Kibandi, this is the first time I have left my own shack, and my masks, of course it's not for me to put an end to him, Tembé-Essouka never kills, he liberates, you must decide, you just need to catch his harmful double who is hiding out in the forest now, he knows his time is almost up, I have used my special powers to immobilise him, if you lay hands on this animal you'll be able to do what you want with his master, his death won't be on your conscience, because you'll only have attacked an animal, he told us exactly where the old rat was hiding, they thanked him, gave him a white mule, a red cockerel and a sack of cowries, the sorcerer refused to spend the night in the village, he would return to Lekana by night, the village headman tried to persuade him, 'sleep here tonight, Venerable Tembé-Essouka, it's dark now, we value your great wisdom', the sorcerer answered, 'Honourable Leader, your words warm my heart, but the blind man has no need of the light of day, I must now return to my hut, my masks await me, don't worry about me, thank you for these gifts', he grabbed the red cockerel by its feet , tied his sack of cowries to the mule's back, and set off home

the next day, the chief citizen of Mossaka called an extraordinary meeting of the elders, an urgent decision was taken, to catch Papa Kibandi unawares, so twelve strong men were appointed to go out into the forest and track down the rat, the twelve strong men armed themselves with 12-bore rifles, poisoned arrows, they circled the part of the bush where Tembé-Essouka had said the rat was, wiped out all the rats they could find, at the foot of a paradise flower they discovered a rat hole, covered over with dead leaves, they dug and they dug for a full half hour till they'd cornered the old beast, who could scarcely move, perhaps he knew his time was up, he couldn't escape this time, he bared his teeth, flashed his incisors threateningly, for once it didn't work, he inspired pity now, not fear, an amber coloured liquid dribbled from his mouth, at this one of the twelve strong men aimed his arrow, let it fly at the beast, he squealed as a liquid as white as palm wine spurted from him, a second arrow shot his brains to pieces, then they took up their rifles, these twelve strong men, and peppered the creature with bullets, just to make sure on returning to the village, the twelve strong men heard, to their surprise, of the death of Papa Kibandi, no one went to the dead man's house, the old man's corpse was laid out in the living room, its staring eyes flipped back in its head, the tongue, a dark indigo blue, lolling towards the right ear, the corpse already rotting, a pestilential smell filled the air, and towards the end of the day as darkness began to fall, Mama Kibandi and my young master rolled the corpse in palm leaves and carried it deep into the forest, buried it in a field of banana trees, crept back into the village, packed a few things, and stole away at break of day, without a trace, following the line of the horizon till they arrived here in Séképembé, I was already here, I had gone on ahead, as soon as I'd seen my young master's double come to tell me they were leaving the village in the north, I knew I must make my way south, to a village named Séképembé, so that is how, through no choice of our own, we came to live in this village, a foster village where we ought even so to have been able to lead a normal life

How Mama Kibandi joined
Papa Kibandi in the
other world

it was strange to see my young master grinding roots with his incisors, sharper than those of an ordinary human, I even wondered if he was going to spend his entire adolescence eating nothing but bulbs, but in the end he accepted the death of his father, living here in Séképembé broadened their horizons, the distance between them and the north helped them put the past behind them, and with it the memory of how the people of Mossaka, aided by the sorcerer, Tembé-Essouka, had wiped out Papa Kibandi, it was clear that Mama Kibandi and my master now hoped to start a new life, it seems only yesterday they moved here, the locals welcomed them as they would any outsider, inviting them in, they moved into a hut made of gaboon planks, with a straw roof, which admittedly was on the edge of the village, but only because there was no land left in the heart of Séképembé, the next question was work, my master became apprentice carpenter to an old man to whom Mama Kibandi paid a modest sum, the old carpenter became almost like a father to Kibandi, who called him 'Papa', he never dared use his real name, Mationgo, this man reminded him of his real father, probably because of his stooping posture, his chameleon-like gait, 'Papa' Mationgo recognised my master as an intelligent, inquisitive young man, Kibandi quickly mastered the subtler points of carpentry, there was no need for the old man to repeat things endlessly, though he did begin to have his doubts about the young apprentice, who, although he followed his instructions to the letter, never failed to amaze him, by updating 'Papa' Mationgo's outmoded work methods, climbing up on to roofs with unusual ease, the old man was dumbfounded when one day, feeling ill, he put my master in charge of making the wooden roof structure for a farm, young Kibandi managed to make the ties, the laterals, the ridgepoles, the cross ridges, the boarding, the beams for the ridge, croup and semi-croup, which was not within the grasp of your average apprentice, and my master even showed the old man how to put up a metal roof frame, before that 'Papa' Mationgo had only ever dealt with wooden frames, in fact everything was just going perfectly between the two humans, I was the one, really, who aroused 'Papa' Mationgo's suspicions, and I know the old man died quite convinced that there was something odd about his apprentice, one day I went for a little wander round the back of the workshop, my master was busy sawing a plank, I heard 'Papa' Mationgo's hesitant tread, he undid his trousers, began pissing against the workshop wall, and when he turned round his eyes met mine, he picked up a large stone lying at his feet, and almost brought me down, the stone landed only a few centimetres away, but the days of his youth were gone, he had lost his aim, I took off in the direction of the river and a few moments later he told my master he believed the porcupines of Séképembé had lost their fear of mankind, that there were too many of them, that the hunters needed to deal with them, that one of these days he might well kill one himself, and eat it with a few green bananas, he swore he would make a trap, Kibandi stopped sawing his wood at that, and answered calmly, 'Papa Mationgo, the porcupine you saw wasn't from Séképembé, believe me', and the old man faltered and gave him a long look, then said in a resigned voice, 'I see, I see, Kibandi, my son, I see, I suspected as much, I must say, but I won't say a word, in any case, I'm just an old wreck myself, a bit of old scrap, I don't want any trouble with people before I leave this world, because I'm going to die any day now' a few years later, before taking his final leave of this life, 'Papa' Mationgo handed over his work tools to my master, Kibandi felt as though his own father had just died all over again, at that time he was seventeen years old, and in spite of his youth, he had learned everything there was to know about roofing, he had more work than any other artisan in the neighbourhood, most of the new huts in Séképembé had roof frames made by him, and when necessary, he would go to the cemetery and stand in silence before the tomb of 'Papa' Mationgo, I would see him sobbing as though at the graveside of his own parent, I was only a few hundred metres away from the cemetery, I knew too, that the noise behind me was coming from my master's other self, I didn't turn round for fearing of meeting the eye of the creature with no mouth, the other self was getting more and more agitated, he slept in the workshop, wandered dewy-eyed along the river bank, climbed trees, I sometimes wondered how he managed to eat, since he had no mouth, and, since I had never seen him snacking, I had to conclude that either it was my master who ate for him, or that the other self must eat by means of a different orifice, I'll leave you to guess which, my dear Baobab for twelve years, poor Mama Kibandi had woven mats which she sold to the locals, she did quite good business, and whenever it was market day in one of the neighbouring villages, Louboulou, Kimandou, Kinkosso or Batalébé, mother and son would go with their wares, Kibandi would spend his holidays in these remote little places, with Mama Kibandi's friends, who were traders like her, leaving me alone with his other self, I didn't much like it when he went away, I felt it upset the harmony between us, I didn't come out of my hiding place, I ate only the supplies my master's other self brought me, thus nights passed, and days passed, my thoughts turned to Kibandi, not that there was any cause for worry, I knew exactly what he was doing during these absences, which lasted only a few weeks, the other self kept nothing from me, I knew, for example, that my master had had his first sexual experience in Kinkosso, with the famous Biscouri, a woman twice his age, a most curvaceous widow, with a cumbersome behind and a rather excessive appetite for virgin boys, the moment she set eyes on one, she'd bound up to him, and pester him, she was well known for it in Kinkosso, she'd hang around after him, talk sweetly to him, prepare food for him, some parents even encouraged her, but widow Biscouri didn't like actually to be offered a virgin boy, she liked to be able to choose her stallion herself, even if he was skinny as a rake, like my master, she had her own technique for snaring innocents, first of all she'd set up a conversation, along the lines of 'I know your mother, boy, she's a fine woman', and then she'd wrap her arms around him and suddenly thrust her hand between his legs, grabbing his intimate parts and then cry 'my god, you've got something there, boy, you're set up for life with that thing' and she'd laugh, and hastily explain 'it's ok, I was only joking, my boy, come on, follow me, I'll make you our finest local dish, the *ngul'mu mako*', but people still felt that Biscouri was the least catastrophic solution to the problem of introducing a boy to sex, now my master did not enjoy this experience, he always felt that Biscouri's excessive ardour had paralysed him, so that he had remained completely passive, as though he were being raped, from then on he began seeing local prostitutes, having got the idea that a woman would only perform the sexual act gently if she was being paid for it, and when he went on holiday to surrounding villages, he would break into his savings and go to the roughest areas, find a different partner every evening, get drunk with a working girl, then return to Séképembé with empty pockets, now Mama Kibandi was no fool, she had a good idea that my master had started seeing women, and she was confident that one day her son would present her with a future daughter-in-law, or people would come knocking at their door with a pregnant daughter

I remember, too, the day Mama Kibandi came across my master sitting in front of the hut reading the Bible, someone had given it

to him in Kinkosso, a religious person who wanted to persuade
him to take up the way of the Lord because he'd seen him in
the prostitutes' area, a sign that my master was a lost sheep, a
sinner who must be guided away from the path to hell, before
this servant of the Lord had had time to discover that he was in
fact illiterate, Kibandi had taken the book and vanished, and
the man in the cassock never realised what a favour he had
done my master, for the first few weeks he didn't open the book,
he left it lying by his bed until it was covered with a layer of
dust, and one evening, unable to sleep, he finally picked it up,
opened it up in the middle, brought it up close to his eyes, drew
a long breath, smelled the pleasant smell of the page, and when
he opened his eyes the light of the storm lantern fell across the
words, and stripped them of their mystery, forming a kind of
halo around each letter, and each phrase began to move, flowing
like a river, he never knew when exactly his lips began to move,
to read, he didn't even know he was turning the pages fast, that
his eyes were flicking from left to right without his feeling any
giddiness, the words were suddenly alive, representing reality,
and he imagined God, and that mysterious vagabond, Jesus,
he would never stop reading, and for the next few days he did
not sleep, he'd fall on the book the minute he got in from the
workshop he'd built behind their hut, Mama Kibandi couldn't
hide her astonishment, she was amused by her son's behaviour,
she wondered why the young man was so concerned to conceal
his ignorance, after all, just because you had a book in your
hands didn't mean you were educated, and she treated it as a
joke, considering my master had never set foot inside a school,
so he couldn't read, and another day, infuriated by my master's
new activity, she glanced at the book he was going through, as

though she too could devour it, her son seemed very focussed, he murmured phrases, traced the lines on the page with the index finger of his right hand, it must have been that day, surely, that she realised Kibandi had to have a double and that his father must have made him drink the *mayamvumbi* in Mossaka from then on my master just had to be reading, he brought all sorts of books back to the house, books he'd bought in neighbouring villages, he placed them in a corner of his workshop, there were some in the bedroom too, most of the books had lost their covers, he spent hours in the library of the church of St Jospeh in the village of Kimondou, and when he wasn't in the workshop or working on site in a neighbouring village, he would spend the entire day reading, it was around this time that I too began to pick out letters among the thoughts passing through my mind, whole words even, it was fun identifying the letters, knowing that somewhere among them there must be a word, before long I could recite what my master read, several times I caught myself muttering aloud to myself, and then I reached the conclusion that for once men really did have a head start on us animals, because they could set down their thoughts, their imaginings on paper, and it was around the same time that curiosity drove me from my hiding place, I went into my master's workshop while he was out with his mother at the market in Séképembé, fell upon the pile of books, I wanted to be sure that I could really recognise the words floating round in my mind like little silver-winged dragonflies, my master had put the Bible by his work tools, as though to consecrate them, I took it and opened it at random, I read several chapters, I discovered some extraordinary stories, like the ones I told you about at the beginning of my confession, I also found some other books, I didn't need to read them all, my master would do that for me, I scuttled off before nightfall, in case Kibandi and his mother found me there, I don't know what would have happened then

I need to find the right words, to explain to you about Mama Kibandi's weak heart, she had always tried to conceal her illness from her son, my master only discovered it when they were living at Séképembé, it got much worse after our twelfth year here, she was at death's door with every crisis, she'd lie still as a corpse for hours, then suddenly, just when you thought she must surely have given up the ghost, she'd breathe in, hold it, then breathe out sharply, murmur something like 'I won't let this cursed illness get me, oh no, I'm a healthy woman, my ancestors are protecting me, every night, every day, I call their names, dear Kong-Dia-Mama, Moukila-Massengo, Kengé-Moukila, Mam'Soko, Nzambi Ya Mpungu, Tata Nzambi, they'll give me a new heart, a heart that beats faster than this old wreck smouldering away beneath my ribs', but what could the ancestors do for a heart that slithered and rumbled and faltered, what could they do for a vital muscle that had contracted, and only supplied blood to half the body, there was nothing to be done, dear Baobab, perhaps they could have seen off a fever, a bladder burn, bilharzia, a flesh wound, a headache, but the heart was something else, Mama Kibandi knew it, the slightest effort tired her out, she hadn't gone out selling her mats for a year now, my master gave up working too, and when I went into the workshop I noticed spiders' webs, dusty books, work tools stowed away in a corner, Kibandi hadn't been up on the roof of a house for months, Mama Kibandi kept telling him to get back to work, my master hardly listened, he stopped visiting the prostitutes in Kinkosso, he watched over his mother, gave her mixtures to drink that turned her lips bright red, he stopped leaving the house, till the day Mama Kibandi went to join Papa Kibandi in the other world, now several weeks before this, as though she had known exactly the hour and date of her departure, and probably because she was taken aback by her son's strange behaviour, suddenly becoming an avid reader, a man of letters, you might say, she again told my master he must not disobey her, must not go down the same path as the late Papa Kibandi, or he might end up the same way, and the young man promised, swore three times on the name of his ancestors, it was a great big lie, it would probably have been better to tell her the truth, because the instant he swore on the blood of his ancestors, a fart of incredible fruitiness issued from his butt, and the two of them, he and the dying woman, had to pinch their nostrils, the smell of rotting corpse got so bad in the room they had to leave the door and windows open for thirty days and thirty nights, it only cleared the day the old lady died, a grey Monday, a Monday when even the flies couldn't get off the ground, Séképembé seemed empty, the sky so low a human could almost have plucked a cluster of clouds without even raising his arm, and then, just on the stroke of eleven in the morning, a flock of skeletal sheep appeared from nowhere, trooped around my master's workshop, stopped in front of the hut, covered the courtyard in diarrhoeal excrement, then made off in single file towards the river, while the oldest of them let out a cry like that of an animal being slaughtered in the abattoir, Kibandi rushed into his mother's bedroom, found her lifeless, her face a rictus, her right hand laid upon her left breast, she had probably been counting her final heart beats, before her eyes closed forever, my master went running all round Séképembé like a madman, telling everyone, Mama Kibandi was buried in a place set aside for strangers, a few people came to the funeral, but not enough, because the villagers still considered her and her son 'outsiders, come from the belly of the mountain', even if they'd been living there for aeons, and, my dear Baobab, the way I see it, confidence between humans comes from a shared knowledge of the past, it's not like in our world, a long established group of animals might view the arrival of an unknown beast with suspicion, animals are organised too, I know that from experience, they have their territory, their governor, their rivers, their trees, their paths, it's not only elephants have graveyards, all animals are attached to their own world, but with the monkey cousins it's strange, there's an emptiness, a shadow, an ambiguity about the past which breeds suspicion, even, sometimes, rejection, and that's why not many locals came to Mama Kibandi's burial, after her body had lain for three days and three nights, under a shelter of palm leaves made by my master in his workshop

dear Baobab, I should like you to think of Mama Kibandi as a brave woman, at least, a woman who loved her child, a humble woman who lived in this village, and loved it, who spent her days weaving mats, a woman who maybe won't find rest in the world hereafter, because my master failed to keep his word, from that point on Kibandi lived here alone, he decided to take up carpentry again, I'd hang around outside his workshop, I'd hear him banging away furiously with his tools, sawing away at the wood, I'd see him set off for the next village, work there, come back in the evening, lie down on his bed, open a book and in that silent hut, where Mama Kibandi's shade could still be felt, especially when a cat meowed late in the night or a fruit splashed into the river, my master's other self visited me more and more often, always with his back to me, all I saw was a sad, lost looking shape, I knew now that we were close, very close to the start of our activities, we could begin, now Mama Kibandi's death had relieved my master of the last of his scruples

how last Friday became
black Friday

let me tell you about the day Kibandi came back from his mother's grave, the day when towards the stroke of ten in the evening, I decided to go and sniff around his hut, all afternoon my master's other self had been hanging about, I heard his footsteps, running everywhere, rustling in the undergrowth, plunging into the river, vanishing one moment, popping up again half an hour later, I knew the other self had a message for me, the time for our first mission had come, I grew restless in my lair, I couldn't keep still, Kibandi wanted to see me, smell me, so, at dead of night I went to the workshop, it was so dark I could scarcely see beyond the end of my snout, there was no light in the hut, usually my master read till the early hours, I also noticed that the door was half open, I slid quietly through and found Kibandi stretched out on the last mat his mother had made before she died, it was only half finished, he loved that mat more than anything, I started nibbling his nails, his heels too, he appreciated these signs of affection and woke up, got to his feet, I saw him dress, turning his back so I wouldn't see his genitals, and as I crossed what served as the living room, I stumbled over his other self, stretched out on the ground, we left the hut, while the other self went and lay down on the last mat woven by Mama Kibandi,

I tripped along behind my master, who was walking with his eyes half closed, like a blind man, and we arrived at a place a few hundred metres from the house of Papa Louboto, the brick maker, my master sat down under a mango tree, I could see he was trembling, talking to himself, touching his belly, as though he had a pain there, 'go on then, it's your call' he said to me, pointing towards the hut at the far end of the concession, and seeing me hesitate he repeated his order in a sterner tone, I did as I was told, and round the back of the hut I found a gaping hole, the work, presumably, of some local rodents, I pushed straight through it and found myself in the bedroom of Papa Louboto's daughter, young Kiminou, a light-skinned girl, an adolescent, with a round face, said to be the prettiest girl in Séképembé, four young men had already asked her father for her hand in marriage, and were just waiting for Papa Louboto's decision, due next year, when the girl came of age, here was young Kiminou now, I stopped to admire her beauty for a moment, the pagne scarcely covering her thighs, her breasts within reach, I felt a violent lurch of desire, I was shocked by my own genitals, I who had never done anything improper with a female, not even one of my own species, I swear, I'd never even once felt the itch, it never crossed my mind, unlike certain members of our group at that time, who stooped to such things the moment the old governor's back was turned, they were older than me, these comrades, and then all at once, the day of my first mission, I got this curious bulge between my hind legs, my sex was growing hard, I'd always thought it was only for pissing, just as my rectum was only for defecating, I was suddenly ashamed, and I swear I couldn't tell you to this day what I would do if I found myself face to face with a porcupine of the opposite sex coming on to me, or giving me the come hither, perhaps I'm still a virgin because of being a double, whenever I saw the other members of our community knocking around with females it felt like I was watching something indecent, it was all very hard work, but they got there in the end, they squealed, groaned, clutched at their partner's quills, I always wondered what they were feeling when they waved their paws around as though they were having an epileptic fit and let me tell you something else, the noise of their quills rubbing together really irritated me, anyway, my comrades seemed to be enjoying themselves thoroughly, then suddenly they'd groan and fall into a state of semi-consciousness, even a babe that piddles in his cradle could have caught them bare-handed, then, the day of my first assignment, I discovered that even though my sex was quite indifferent to the attractions of a female porcupine, it immediately reacted to the sight of a naked human of the feminine sex, still my mission was not to try to get it on with this girl, so after a moment's hesitation I set these thoughts aside, and told myself such things were not for me, they were things to be done between members of the same species, and to rid my mind completely of such ideas I tried to think about something completely different, I wondered what had made my master take against the lovely Kiminou, her perfectly formed body perhaps, and once again I brushed aside such considerations with the back of my paw, not wanting to weaken just as I was about to go into action, but deep down, even if I was deliberately making my mind go blank, I couldn't help wondering, and I remembered that Kibandi was one of the four marriage candidates, which had made the whole village laugh, and he wished he'd never asked, I'd seen him two or three times in discussion with Papa Louboto near the market place, one day they drank a glass of palm wine together, the man had spoken with warmth of Mama Kibandi, he said 'she was a really good woman, she'll be remembered many years in this village, believe me, you can be proud of her, and I know she is watching over you', his voice was totally insincere, and Kibandi remembered that Papa Louboto hadn't turned up at his mother's funeral, so he was pretending to be nice to my master in the hope of receiving his gifts as a suitor to his daughter, only to reject him when the moment came, then, when all the candidates had finished talking with the potential father-in-law, each of them went away convinced he was the right man for the job, he was the one Papa Louboto would give his daughter to blindly, now my master wasn't falling for that, he knew he didn't stand a chance, but even so, he gave that swindler everything he owned, everything his mother had given him, special celebration mats, baskets of palm nuts, all his work savings, he remade the man's roof free of charge, you could see in Papa Louboto's eyes a kind of inexhaustible expectation, he went round the village boasting, saying Kibandi was bug ugly, thin as the tack in a photo frame, adding that a woman worthy of the name would never accept Kibandi, but let him dream on, he'd ruin him, take everything off him, down to his underpants, his vests, his rubber sandals, I expect it was frustration and fury drove my master to take on this family, because, let me make it quite clear, dear Baobab, for one human being to eat another you need concrete reasons, jealousy, anger, envy, humiliation, lack of respect, I swear we never once ate someone just for the pleasure of eating, and so, on that memorable night, while young Kiminou slept like an angel, her arms crossed over her chest, I drew a deep breath, took one of my strongest quills, and threw it straight at her right temple, before she could realise what was happening, then a second, she shuddered, in vain she struggled, she was paralysed, I went up to her, heard her muttering nonsense, I started licking the blood as it oozed down her temple, I saw the hole left by my two quills vanish as though by magic, you'd have needed four eyes to see any sign of what had happened, I went into the next room, where the young girl's parents lay sleeping, the father snoring like a clapped out car, the mother with her left arm dangling over the side of the bed, it was not part of my mission to deal with them, so I pushed aside the voice that whispered in my ear, telling me to shoot a couple of quills into Kimouni's parents' temples

the next day, the whole of Séképembé was in shock, Kiminou was dead, and though it was generally agreed she had been eaten, it was assumed to be the result of rivalry between the mother's and father's lines, there was some dispute between the two, out came the scythes, the spears, the axes, the chief of Séképembé managed to calm the two camps, he proposed a trial on the day of the funeral, where the corpse picks out the criminal, Kibandi was half expecting it, dear Baobab, so he was prepared, Papa Kibandi had taught him to get round these things, my master had stuck a palm nut up his rectum just as his progenitor had, back when he was trying to catch out the sorcerer Tembé-Essouka, and the corpse of young Kiminou picked out one of the other marriage candidates instead, and the poor innocent was buried alive with the deceased, with no further trial, because that's how things were done my dear Baobab, the universally dreaded trial by corpse, where the corpse picks out its aggressor, is widely used in these parts, whenever someone dies, the villagers rush to do it, to their minds there's no such thing as a natural death, only the dead can tell the living who caused their death, I expect you'd like to know how it's done, well, four strong men carry the coffin on their shoulders, a sorcerer chosen by the village chief picks up a piece of wood, knocks three times on the casket, and says to the corpse, 'tell us who ate you, show us where the wrongdoer lives, you can't just disappear into the other world without vengeance, come on now, stir yourself, run, fly, cross the mountains, the plains, and if the wrongdoer lives across the Ocean, if he lives up in the stars, we'll seek him out and make him pay for what he has done you and your family', the coffin suddenly starts to move, the four strong bearers get dragged into a devilish sort of dance, they no longer feel the weight of the corpse, they run left and right, often the casket drags them way off into the bush, then brings them hurtling back into the village at breakneck speed, and though they walk on thorns, on shards, they feel no pain, they are not harmed, they plunge into water, but do not drown, they pass through bush fires and are not burned, and once White men came here to watch this practice, so they could put it in a book, they said they were ethnologists, they had difficulty explaining to some of Séképembé's less sophisticated inhabitants quite what an ethnologist was for, I had a good laugh myself, because I could just have speeded things along by saying an ethnologist was someone who discusses other people's customs, which strike them as strange when compared to their own culture, no more no less, but one of the Whites made so bold as to explain to the poor lost souls of this village that the word 'ethnology' came from the Greek word *ethnos*, meaning 'people', therefore what ethnologists study is people, societies, customs, ways of thinking, ways of living, anyone who was bothered by the word 'ethnologist' could simply say 'social anthropologist' , which created still more confusion and most people just went on thinking they were people who were out of work in their own countries or who had come to put satellite dishes in the village so as to watch people, so anyway, there they were, these ethnologists or social anthropologists, they'd been waiting for someone to die, and luckily for them an individual had been eaten here, not by my master, by another guy whose double was a shrew, the ethnologists all cheered 'fantastic, we've got our stiff, he's at the other end of the village, the burial's tomorrow, at last we'll be able to finish that darned book', and they asked if they might carry the coffin themselves, on their shoulders, because they were convinced there was something not quite right about this whole business, that it was really the men who carried the coffin who shook it about so as to get people falsely accused, but the question of whether or not the White men could take part in the ritual divided the village, some sorcerers were opposed to foreigners meddling in Séképembé's affairs, in the end the village chief played diplomat and swore that the rites of the ancestors would still work, even in the presence of the Whites, because the village ancestors are stronger than the Whites, and he convinced everyone that it was a good thing these outsiders would be present during the rite, what's more, they'd mention Séképembé in their book, the village would become world famous, people from many other countries would be inspired by our customs, to the greater glory of the ancestors, and that put an end to the discontent, which transformed into a collective sense of pride, another row almost blew up when it came to choosing one out of the twelve village sorcerers to supervise the ritual, they all wanted to work with the Whites now, when only a few hours earlier such a thing would have been inconceivable, and all the sorcerers began bragging about their family tree, but only one of them was needed, the village chief took twelve cowries, marked one of them with a little cross, put them in a basket, shook them and asked each sorcerer to close his eyes and put his hand inside and take one cowrie at random, the one who drew out the marked cowrie would have the honour of directing the ritual, the suspense lasted until the eleventh cowrie, when one of the sorcerers, who had kept on putting off his turn drew it out, before the envious gaze of all the others, and so, once all these negotiations were complete, the ethnologists or social anthropologists finally lifted the coffin, amid laughter from all the villagers, who seemed not to be concerned that their hilarity might bring shame upon the corpse, and the sorcerer, who was also fighting back guffaws, gave three sharp knocks with his bit of stick, struggled to find words with which to ask the corpse to point out the person who had harmed him, but the deceased understood what was expected of him, as well he might, because in his remarks the sorcerer added, 'be careful not to bring shame on us in front of these White men who have come from afar and think our customs are just one big joke', the corpse didn't need to be asked twice, a light rain began to fall, and when the coffin started jolting forwards, hopping like a baby kangaroo, the ethnologists at the back shouted 'come on now, comrades, stop shaking the damn' coffin, let it move on its own if it's really gonna move' and the other ethnologists replied, 'stop assing around guys, you're the one who's moving it', the corpse started dancing around, speeded up its rhythm, dragged the ethnologists off into a lantana field, then brought them back to the village, pushed them down as far as the river, brought them back up to the village again and the whole mad chase finally came to a halt in front of old Mouboungoulo's hut, with a huge thrust, the coffin broke down the door of the guilty man's hut, drove into his home, an old shrew that stank like a skunk slipped out of the house, circled in the courtyard, then shot off down to the river, the coffin caught it at the first thicket of trees, came down on top of it, and that is how old Mouboungoulou met his death, dear Baobab, and apparently the Whites wrote a long book about the incident, over 900 pages, I don't know whether the village of Séképembé has become world famous, what I do know is that other Whites have turned up since, just to check what the first ones wrote in their book, several of them left empty handed because the locals with harmful doubles were wary of them, and suddenly it seemed like no one ever died when the whites were around, a few corpses refused to go along with the ritual, refused to play the game, or sometimes the villagers would instruct their families, in the event of their death, not to allow their corpses to take part in the ritual in the presence of Whites, who might then go and sully their global reputation, so now, you see, the ritual is practised only with great caution, but the most convincing reason, let me tell you, dear Baobab, came from a guy called Amédée, and the reason I speak of him in the past tense is because he has passed on to the next world, may his soul rest in peace, he was what humans called an educated man, a cultivated man, who had studied for many years, he was respected for it, added to which he had travelled widely, he had been up in a plane several times, one of those noisy birds that rip the sky in two, every time you think it's going to take your head off, apparently Amédée was the most intelligent men in the entire south, not to say in the whole country, but that didn't stop us, we still ate him, as you will soon learn, he claimed that the book written by the first Whites on this question had been published in Europe and translated into several languages, he asserted that it had become a key work of reference for ethnologists and Amédée, who had read it, was harsh in his criticism, saying 'I have never read such a trumped up work, what else can I say, it's a disgraceful book, a book which seeks to humiliate Africans, a tissue of lies by a group of Europeans in search of exoticism, who would like nothing better than for Negroes to continue dressing in leopard skins and living up trees' a breeze is rising now, your leaves fall upon me, it's a pleasant feeling, it's these little things that remind me of the joy of being alive, and looking up at the sky above I think to myself how lucky you have been, to live here, in this place, so close to paradise, where everything is green, here on top of the hill, overlooking the surrounding countryside, the trees all around are bent low towards the ground, while you consider the moods of the sky, with the indifference of one who has seen it all, over the years, compared with you the other vegetable species are mere garden gnomes, you watch over the entire plant world, from here I can hear the river running, splashing down onto a rock further downstream, people from Séképembé hardly ever come here, even if they cut down every single species in the bush, no one would lay a finger on you, the villagers respect the baobabs, I know it hasn't always been so, I know things have been said about you, I can read in the veins of your bark, some of them are scars, some madmen in the village tried to finish you off, and in a destructive frenzy, for porcupine's sake, they set about you with an axe, to chop you up for firewood, they said you hid the horizon, you blocked out the light of day, well they didn't succeed, their saw buckled in the face of your legendary resistance, then they made do with gaboon planks for their coffins, their houses, the same wood my master used to make roof structures, and some villagers believe you have a soul, that you protect this region, that if you disappeared it would be a bad thing, fatal, even, for our region, that your sap is as sacred as the holy water in the village church, that you are the guardian of the forest, that you have existed since the dawn of time, that's why, perhaps, the sorcerers use your bark to heal the sick, others say that a word with you is a word with the ancestors, 'sit at the foot of a baobab tree, and given time, you'll see the whole universe pass before you', our old porcupine used to say, he told us that at that time the baobabs could talk, respond to humans, punish them, whip them with their branches when the monkey cousins took up arms against the plant world and in those days he went on, the baobabs could move about, find themselves a more comfortable spot where they could take better root, some of them came from far, far away, they would pass other baobabs going the other way because one always tends to think that the soil elsewhere is better than one's native soil, that life is easier elsewhere, I think about those days, when everything was on the move, and distance was no obstacle, nowadays no one would believe the governor, no man bloated with reason and clogged with prejudice would ever have the idea that a tree with its feet planted once and for all in the ground could move about, after all, the incredulous soul would retort straightaway, 'and why not the mountains while we about it, eh, they could go walk about too, say how d'you do at the crossroads, talk about the wind and the weather, swap addresses, exchange family news, it's all just twaddle, that is', but I believe it, for once I'm with our governor, they weren't legends, it wasn't just twaddle, he was right, and I know that you must have moved about too, you must have fled other lands where the desert threatened to erode, regions where you can count each drop of rain that falls, you left your family, returned to the rainy region, you must deliberately have chosen the most fertile spot in this country, I don't know of any other baobab round here, I would love to trace your genealogy, find out which tree you're descended from, and where your earliest ancestors lived, but perhaps I've strayed too far from the subject of my confessions, talking of you, it must be the human in me speaking, in fact I learned my sense of digression from men, they never go straight to the point, open brackets they forget to close there's a certain kind of person I really don't like, like the educated young man called Amédée, whom we ate, he was only about thirty, he was the one who had read the book in which the ethnologists or social anthropologists wrote about the practice of the corpse denouncing whoever had harmed him, the reason I mention it is because if there's one person whose disappearance I really don't regret it's that young man, he was such a show-off, a braggart of the first order, he thought he was most intelligent person in the village, in the region, not to say the whole country, he wore Terylene suits, sparkly ties, the kind of shoes you wear if you work in an office, those dens of idleness where men sit down, pretend to read papers and put off till tomorrow what they should be doing today, Amédée walked around with his chest puffed out, just because he'd studied for years, simply because he'd visited countries where it snows, let me tell you this, whenever he came to Séképembé to visit his parents, the young girls on heat went running after him, even married women cheated on their husbands, they'd bring him things to eat on the quiet, round the back of his father' s hut, they'd wash his dirty linen for him, the guy went round doing things he shouldn't have all over the place with married women and the young women on heat, down by the river, in the grass, in the fields, behind the church, near the cemetery, I couldn't believe my eyes, true, he was handsome, athletic, and he certainly spent a lot of time on his looks, almost like a human of the feminine sex, such coquettishness had never been seen before in our village, and when he went to bathe in the river he'd spend hours gazing at himself in the water, rubbing in scented oils, and where the river grew calm, like a mirror, conspiring with his vanity, he admired his own reflection, until one day he almost drowned, when, leaning far over, so as to be able to see the whole length of his body, he stepped onto a stone covered with moss, and splash! bless my quills, he tripped, and ended up in the water, but luckily for him he knew how to swim, and in less than no time he got across to the other side, laughing like a moron, the bathers all applauded, and to celebrate the day he almost died, he picked a red hibiscus flower, threw it into the river, watched it follow the current, disappearing in a tangle of ferns and lilies, which is why people from this village don't say 'red hibiscus' now, they call it 'flower of Amédée'

the worst thing was, Amédée would criticise the old folk out loud, calling them ignorant old fools, the only ones whom he spared were his own parents, saying that if his parents had been able to go to school they would have been as intelligent as he was, because that's where he got his intelligence from, and at sunrise each day, he'd sit under a tree, reading great thick books in tiny print, the big show-off, novels usually, oh, I'm sure you've never seen a novel, I don't suppose anyone's ever sat beneath your shade reading a novel, well you're not missing anything, but just to keep it simple, and not pollute your spirit, I'll tell you this, novels are books written by men to recount things which are untrue, they'll say it all comes from their imagination, there are some novelists who would sell their own mothers or fathers to steal my porcupine destiny, draw inspiration from it, write a story in which I'd have an rather less than glorious role, make me look like low life, let me tell you this, human beings find life so boring, they need novels so they can invent other lives for themselves, by diving into one of these books, dear Baobab, you can take off round the world, leave the bush in the blink of an eye, turn up in a distant country, meet foreign people, strange animals, porcupines with even murkier pasts than mine, I was often intrigued, hiding there in my bush, hearing Amédée talk to the young girls about the things in his books, and the girls looked at him with more respect and consideration because for monkey cousins, if you've read a lot of books it gives you the right to boast, to look down on others, and people who've read a great deal seem to talk all the time, especially about the things in their books that are most difficult to understand, they want other people to know they've read things, so Amédée would tell the young girls all about a wretched old man who went deep sea fishing and had to battle all alone with a huge fish, if you ask me this huge fish was the harmful double of a fisherman who was jealous of the old guy's experience, our erudite young friend also talked about another old man who liked to read love stories and went to help a village to wipe out a wild beast that was terrorising the region, I'm sure the beast was the harmful double of a villager in that distant land, and it was also Amédée who told them several times over the story of a guy who flew about on a magic carpet, a patriarch who founded a village called Macondo, and all his descendents were afflicted by a kind of curse and were born half-man, half-animal, with snouts, and pig's tails, I'm convinced these must have been cases of harmful doubles, and if I remember correctly, he told stories about some weird guy who went round fighting windmills, or, in a similar vein a poor unfortunate officer in a desert camp sitting waiting for reinforcements, and then again the old colonel waiting for a letter and his veteran's pension, living in abject poverty with his sick wife, all their hopes pinned on their fighting cock, that cock was their one ray of hope, it must have been a peaceful double of some kind, well, I won't go on, and then, to give the girls a scare, because they get a thrill out of stories of rape, blood and murder, Amédée told them about a sexually impotent gangster who raped someone using a corn cob, somewhere in south America, and in the same breath he'd tell them the tragic tale of a double murder in the bizarrely named Rue de la Morgue, and since it was about a young woman who was strangled and stuck head first down a chimney, the girls shrieked with horror when Amédée added that behind the building where this drama had taken place, in a little courtyard, was a second corpse, that of an old lady, who'd had her throat cut and her head chopped off, and some of the girls left at this point, and only came back when Amédée had unravelled the mystery of this dread murder, by following the brilliant analysis of the investigator, but actually what thrilled them most was the tale of a beautiful woman called Alicia, in some respects, it occurred to me that Amédée was making fun of my master, Kibandi, here, talking about him in veiled terms, the young man would say things like, 'let us now leave the world of Edgar Allen Poe, let me take you far away to Uruguay, and Horacio Quiroga', and then he'd delight in describing Alicia, a shy, blonde, angelic young woman, he would say, and all the girls would sigh 'ahhhh', and the young man of letters would say that Alicia loved her husband Jordan, but he was a hard man, they loved each other though they could not have been more different, they walked round arm in arm, but their marriage would last three months, no longer, that was their destiny, autumn came, clouds darkened their idyll, like a curse, almost, come to blight their love, then things got even dicier when Alicia caught a kind of flu which she couldn't shake off, she lay in her bed, unable to leave it, in terrible pain, each day she grew thinner, the life seemed to seep out of her, and nothing was as it had been, though her husband tried to heal her, and at this point in the story, when Amédée came to paint a picture of the couple's house, a note of terror began to creep in, joy turned to fear, Amédée dropped his voice, and described the home of Jordan and Alicia, 'inside, inside the glacial brilliance of stucco, the bare walls affirmed the sensation of unpleasant coldness, whenever someone walked through the rooms, their footfall echoed throughout the house, as if long abandonment had increased its resonance', no one knew what was wrong with Alicia, different doctors tried, and failed to cure her, none of the various medicines worked, in the end Alicia died, and after her death, the maid came in to strip the bed, and discovered to her amazement two bloodstains on the feather pillow beneath her head, the maid tried to get them out, and finding the feather pillow surprisingly heavy, she asked the young widow, Jordan, to help, they placed it on the table, Jordan set about cutting it up with a knife, 'the top feathers floated off and the maid opened her mouth wide and clutched at her head wrap and shrieked with horror', read Amédée, in a dark, serious tone, and since the girls of Séképembé still hadn't understood what Jordan and the maid had found under the feather pillow, Amédée at last revealed it to them, weighing each word as he said 'underneath, among the feathers, slowly waving his velvet paws, sat a monstrous beast, a living, slimy ball,' and it was this beast which, over five days and nights, had sucked out Alicia's blood with its trunk, and I did wonder whether Alicia was perhaps an initiate, a human being who'd been eaten by her own harmful double, hidden in the feather pillow

one day my master said to me 'you see, we have to have that young man, he thinks too much of himself, he tells people stupid stories, it seems he puts it about that I'm sick, and that there's a beast that eats me every evening', and we waited till the dry season holiday, when he was due back from Europe with his box of books, and one day Amédée walked past my master's shack, he saw Kibandi sitting outside with an esoteric book in his hands, Amédée said, 'my dear sir, I'm so glad to see you read from time to time', my master didn't answer, the young man went on, 'if I'm not mistaken, you seem rather thin to me, and remind me of an unfortunate character in *Stories of Love, Madness and Death*, things go from bad to worse for you, year after year, it's not even your mother's death that's got you into this state, is it, I strongly recommend you see a doctor in town, I hope there isn't a beast hidden under your pillow feeding off your blood through its trunk, if there is, there's still time to burn the pillow, to kill the beast hidden within', once again, my master didn't react, he thought our village intellectual was raving, mixing up real people and characters in the books he'd brought back from Europe, and Kibandi went on reading his own book, which was about more important things than the things in Amédée's books, and when the young man had walked on by Kibandi took one last look at him and said to himself 'we'll see which one of us grows so thin he looks like the rib of a roof frame, I'm not one of those little maids you tell your stories to'

Amédée went out at dawn for his morning walk in the bush, wearing nothing but a pair of shorts, whistling as he walked down to the river bank, where he dipped his feet in the water, stretched out on the bank and began reading his books full of lies, my master had told me to spy on him, see what he was getting up to all alone there, make sure the young man didn't also have a double who could make trouble for us while we were seeing to him, it was an unnecessary precaution, dear Baobab, they get so narrow-minded for porcupine's sake, all those guys who go off to Europe, they think stories of doubles only exist in African novels, which, instead of setting them thinking, just makes them laugh, they would rather think rationally, as the white men's science teaches them, and the rational thoughts they've been taught say that every phenomenon has a scientific explanation, and when Amédée saw me coming out from a clump of bushes near the river, for porcupine's sake, he yelled furiously, 'out of my sight, filthy beast, ball of prickles, before I turn you into pâté and eat you with chili and manioc', I ballooned till I was ten times my normal size, I was almost exploding, my eyes were popping out of my head, I rattled my quills, whirled round in circles, saw him grab a piece of wood, meaning to smack me on the head, which reminded me of Papa Mationgo back when my master was his apprentice, I did an about turn, looked for escape from impending slaughter, shot off into the bushes I'd emerged from, Amédée stepped towards me, I knew these bushes better than he did, so I rolled all the way down on some dead leaves and found myself at the bottom of the hill, he threw the stick of wood, it landed a few inches from my snout, and when I found my master half an hour later, I told him how the fellow had insulted us, had almost killed us with his piece of wood, Kibandi kept his cool, 'don't worry about it' he reassured me, 'there's nothing he can to do harm us, I haven't been to Europe myself, but I'm not ignorant, with the *mayamvumbi* you don't need to go to school to learn to read and write, it opens your mind, channels the intelligence, he won't be getting his plane back to Europe, that's for sure, he's ours now, his grave's as good as dug, as far as I'm concerned he's been dead a long while, but he doesn't realise, because the Whites don't teach that kind of thing in their schools' at midnight, in heavy rain, we made our way to Amédée's little hut, next to his parents', we had left my master's other self stretched out on the last mat Mama Kibandi ever wove, blinding streaks of lightning flashed across the sky, Kibandi sat down under a tree, signalled to me to go on ahead while he took a good glug of *mayamvumbi*, I didn't take much bidding, I was angry with our little genius myself, I went and scrabbled furiously at the earth under the door of his hovel, to make a way in, and the rain, which by now was falling in torrents, made my task easier, so that in no time I managed to dig a hole so deep that even two fat, idle porcupines could get through without any problem, and once I was inside I saw a lighted candle, the fool had forgotten to blow it out, he was sleeping on his belly, I crept silently forward, came level with the bamboo bed, I don't know why, I suddenly felt afraid, but I managed to control it, I stood up on two legs and clutched at the side of the bed, I was between his two spread legs now, I tensed, so as to find the strongest quill from among the tens of thousands I might have used at that moment, and zap, I released it, it landed right in the back of his neck, the quill almost penetrated all the way into the brain which had so annoyed my master, and as a result, annoyed me also, Amédée had no time to wake up, he was seized with a series of spasms and hiccups while I fell upon his body to remove the quill with my incisors, I took it out, I licked the blood till no trace of my act remained, I saw the little hole close again, just like when I had seen to Papa Louboto's daughter, the lovely young Kimouni, I jumped down onto the ground, but before I left I went up close to the candle because I wanted to burn down his hut, and then I said to myself there was no point doing that, I shouldn't exceed the limits of my mission, Kibandi would have been angry with me, I glanced out of curiosity at the title of the last book the bookworm had been reading before going to bed, *Extraordinary Stories*, sleep had pulled him into the world of these stories, it was another one of those books he took his lies from, to tell the village girls, now he could go and tell them to the phantoms, it's another world there, another universe, they never believe anything, to start with they don't believe in the end of their physical bodies, they resent us for going on living, the Earth for going on turning, and that's why, instead of going up to heaven, they wander the earth, restless shades, hoping to live again, I mean phantoms won't just swallow whatever you tell them

Amédée's funeral was one of the most moving ever seen in Séképembé, in marked contrast to that of the late lamented Mama Kibandi, the crowd around his mortal remains seemed to consist entirely of young girls, they had all summoned their girlfriends from neighboring villages to come and pay due homage to this exceptional being, the pride of Séképembé, of the entire region, not to say country, and everyone wanted to know what had happened to our resident intellectual, some said he'd read too many books brought from Europe, others demanded we carry out the ritual whereby the corpse identifies the criminal, Amédée's parents opposed this idea because, as they recalled, their son didn't believe in such things, it would be an offence to parade his corpse around the village, so they accepted his death, they buried the young man with two boxes of books, some of them were still in their wrappings, with prices in the currency they use in Europe, and in the funeral speech, made this time by the priest from the town, and not by one of the village sorcerers, whom they suspected couldn't speak Latin, the man of God recalled how this young man of letters had pushed back the tide of ignorance, demonstrating that the pages of a book offer a new freedom, restore our humanity, he spoke in Latin, read out a few pages of *Extraordinary Stories*, put the book to one side, picked up a brand new Bible, placed it on the coffin and concluded, in a bleating voice, 'may this book, dear Amédée, guide you along the unfathomable way of the Lord, that you may at last come to see that the most extraordinary story of all is that of the creation of Man by God, a story contained in the pages of the Holy Book I give you now, for your journey to the other world, amen' my master may have been a quiet tempered man, but he was not someone to pick a quarrel with, I only saw him get into an argument once or twice, there was that time with old Moudiongui, the palm wine tapper, probably the best palm wine tapper in Séképembé, they knew each other very well, he and my master, I would never have imagined that one day I would find myself dealing with a loser like him, his whole life revolved around palm wine, he could draw *mwengué*, the finest wine to be got from a palm tree, the village women were crazy for it since it was sweeter than any other wine, but the bad thing about the *mwengué* is that you don't know you're getting drunk, you drink cup after cup and don't realize you're cackling like a hyena, and it's only when you try to get up you find you can't control your legs, you walk all crooked, like a crab, everyone busts out laughing, saying 'there's another one who's been at Moudiongui's *mwengué*', and my master had got into the bad habit of mixing a bit of *mwengué* with his initiation drink, to make it less bitter, so now he would only drink it when it was mixed with old Moudiongui's palm wine, so every morning the old loser stopped by Kibandi's hut to drop off a pint of palm wine, he spoke fondly of Mama Kibandi and remarked how quickly time passed, in fact this was to make Kibandi feel sorry for him so he'd give him more money, my master paid no attention, handed him a crumpled note, Kibandi was convinced that the palm wine added that extra something to his *mayamvumbi*, now old Moudiongui was becoming unreliable, he'd get into a sulk for nothing, sometimes Kibandi had to go and wake him to get him to go out into the bush and fetch the palm wine and, taking advantage of my master's dependence, the old man put up the price as he felt like it, take it or leave it, 'if you don't like it, go and fetch your own *mwengué*, otherwise, pay my price, end of discussion', Moudiongui claimed that *mwengué* was getting increasingly hard to come by, that the palm trees in our region had stopped producing this special wine, that my master would have to make do with normal palm wine, and one day the old man brought back some *mwengué*, as usual, my master tasted it, he had a moment of doubt, he realized it wasn't real *mwengué*, the old man was tricking him, he said nothing, just called me one evening and said, 'right, tomorrow at dawn when the plains grow bright, go follow that bastard palm wine tapper, he's acting strange, I can feel it, go and see how he works' and I followed him first thing next morning, I saw him vanish into the forest, till he reached a place where there's nothing but palm trees, as far as the eye can see, and I saw him climb to the top of a palm tree where he'd hung his gourds the day before, he took them down, they were full, he climbed down, he sat at the foot of the tree, took out a small bag from his pocket, I caught him pouring sugar into the palm wine he'd just drawn, and since he was mad at my master he even spat into the gourd, muttering angrily, and I reported this back to Kibandi later, so when the palm wine tapper turned up at Kibandi's house to offer him this nasty brew, he had the truth flung in his face, I heard them arguing, old Moudiongui was desperate to sell his palm wine, my master replied that it wasn't real *mwengué*, they called each other all the names under the sun, old Moudiongui insulted my master, 'nothing but a bag of bones, you are, you're dead already, you're jealous of my trade because you're only a poor carpenter, you couldn't even climb up a mango tree, you're a crazy guy, a *maniongi*, a *ngébé*, a *ngouba yak o pola*', all insults in *bembé*, Kibandi didn't answer, he just said to the palm wine tapper, 'let's just see, shall we, who's the *maniongi*, the *ngébé*, the *ngouba yak o pola* around here', old Moudiongui said, just as he was leaving, 'what will we see, then, you're a nobody you are, don't expect me to give you *mwengué* from now on, old dry bones, go join your mother in the graveyard'

I left my master with his other self , the two of them lying on the last mat Mama Kibandi ever wove, at break of day I returned to the foot of the same palm tree where I'd caught the palm wine tapper mixing sugar in the gourd and spitting into it, slowly I climbed to the top and hid there, a few centimeters from the hanging gourds, which were filled to overflowing with palm wine, the bees were already having a party up there, I saw Moudiongui arrive, he seemed quite anxious, his eyes darting about, he couldn't understand how my master had found out about his little fiddle, I saw him arranging the ropes he used to climb up to the top of the palm tree, up he climbed, up and up, but halfway up he paused to look about him, as though to make sure no one had spotted him, then, reassured, he went on climbing, he was almost at the gourds, and when he looked up, bless my quills, found himself looking into my dark, glistening eyes, it was too late for him, I'd already fired two of my quills, hitting him full in the face, the old man slipped, tried in vain to grab the branch of a paradise tree just next to the palm tree, I heard him fall, and land like a sack of potatoes down below, his legs and arms spread wide, the villagers found him there a day later, eyes wide open, his face locked in a rictus, and everyone agreed he had grown too old to tap palm wine, he should really have retired long ago, and now a young person from Séképembé must be trained up to take over his work the problem with Youla was he owed my master money, I think this must be one of our most heartbreaking episodes to date because now I really think about it, it was the thing which ultimately brought about Kibandi's downfall, but I need to tell you the whole thing more slowly, after completing this mission I felt uneasy, I kept seeing the victim's face, his innocence, I really felt Kibandi had gone a bit too far this time, but then did I have a right to tell him how I felt, it's not for a double to judge or argue, and certainly not let his own remorse get in the way of things, and as far as I was concerned this was one of the most gratuitous acts we had committed, Youla was father of a happy family, a modest peasant with no education and not much success, he had a wife who loved him and had just had a child by him, a baby whose eyes were barely yet open, and then, one day, I don't know why, this business of the debt between him and Kibandi cropped up, Youla had been to see him to borrow money, a ridiculously small sum which he said he'd pay back the next week, it seems he wanted to buy some medicine for his child and swore he would pay back the full sum by the agreed day, he grovelled, went down on bended knee, wept, because no one had been prepared to lend him this pitiful sum, Kibandi did him the favour, though his own finances were dwindling from

year to year now that he'd given up carpentry, and the notes he
gave Youla were so dirty and crumpled, they looked like they'd
come straight out of the bin, and a week went by, no visitor to
the hut, another week, still Youla didn't show up, he'd dropped
out of circulation, my master thought correctly that he must have
done a runner, so he went to his home two months later, and told
him if he didn't give him his money back things would get nasty
between them, and as the man was drunk that day he began
sniggering and insulting Kibandi, telling him to drag his skinny
frame off someplace else, which of course did not please my
master, who said 'you can find the money to get yourself drunk
but you can't pay your debts', and when Youla just laughed harder,
Kibandi added dryly, out loud, 'people with no money shouldn't
have children', Youla indulged in the remark ' I'm not even sure
I do owe you money, do I, maybe you've got the wrong person,
now get out of my yard', his wife then joined in, telling him to
get lost, or she'd summon an elder of the village, and when my
master got back home, feeling vexed, I saw him talking aloud to
himself, cursing, I knew then that things were going to go badly
wrong for Youla, I had never seen Kibandi in such a state, not
even when that young show-off Amédée had called him a sick
hick, he summoned me straight away, this was urgent, he couldn't
wait, Youla would soon see what my master was made of, and at
midnight, after Kibandi had taken a giant dose of *mayamvumbi*,
this time without mixing it with *mwengué* to sweeten it, we were
all ready to go, my master's other self was coming with us for once,
although I wasn't very clear what his role would be, we came to the
peasant's compound, his house was so run down a donkey could
have got in through the holes in the outside walls, my master sat
down at the foot of a paradise tree, his other self was behind him,

with his back to us, as usual when he was moving about, I walked round the house, ending up in the bedroom, I saw Youla snoring on a mat, with his wife in bed at the far end of the room, I expect it was always like that when the husband was drunk, I crossed the room, went towards the child's room, as soon as I got close to the baby I felt a pang, I wished I could go back home, Kibandi's other self was behind me, I wondered why my master had decided to attack the little babe instead of the man who owed him money, or if it came to that, his wife, who had dared take sides in their argument, my quills grew heavy and reluctant, I told myself I wouldn't be able to shoot, I had never attacked a child before, I needed to find a reason, something to increase my determination and put some fight back into me, but what motive could there be, I couldn't think, then suddenly I said to myself that my master was right, actually, to remind this guy that when you have no money you've no business making children, and I also remembered that the old porcupine used to preach that all men were bad, including children, because 'the tiger's young are born with claws' so we needed to pin some vice on him, find some fault with him that was beyond redemption, I told myself he was a drunkard, and in any case, the poor kid would have a terrible life with this uneducated peasant, I muttered these arguments to myself, in an attempt to sweep away the remorse, as though I could banish the pity which was making my quills wilt, suddenly they perked up, I could feel them starting to whirr, my master's anger was now my anger, as though it was me Youla owed money, and I lost the sense that the creature before me was just an poor innocent thing, I told myself that in fact our action would free him, relieve his suffering, Youla didn't deserve to be a father, being an alcoholic who broke his word, who perhaps owed money to the entire population, and at that moment of reflection I tensed, a firm quill flew out of my back and into the poor child, my master's other self had gone from the room, perhaps he'd been there to give me the strength to do the deed, I quickly left myself, so I wouldn't get upset, what I really didn't want to do was watch the poor innocent child taking leave of this life just because of the stupidity and irresponsibility of his father, that I did not want to see, and yet something about it bothered me, I felt ashamed of my own reflection in the water, I went to the funeral, perhaps hoping for some kind of forgiveness, I heard the poor folk singing their funeral songs, and I wept

in the days shortly after this incident, the image of baby Youla came back to haunt me, I began to fear my own shadow in bright daylight, I imagined the ghost of the baby was hiding behind the next bush, waiting for me, and perhaps that was a weight on my conscience too, and I withdrew into the bush and took stock, I analysed all the facts, the only slightly serious, the rather serious, the serious and above all the very serious, like the death of this child, and the faces of our victims flashed before me, we had already carried out ninety-nine missions, but not the slightest suspicion attached to us at that point, my master always got away with it, thanks to the palm nut he stuffed up his rectum, and I couldn't work out why, out of all our victims, the only one that really stopped me thinking about anything else was this baby of Youla's, it was as though he was spying on us, waiting for us at each bend in the road, and after all, I said to myself, he was only a tiny little human, with no strength, and no power, and I remembered also how the old governor used to warn us that the enemies we should really fear were the tiny ones, and sometimes I told myself that this little baby had a message for me, was trying to tell me to revolt, and all I had to do to break the chain of our missions was to take my own life, or rebel against my master by standing up to him, or disappear without trace, but some force held me back, even though I had the feeling our hundredth mission would be fatal to us, would most certainly cost us our lives, perhaps it was just me worrying, and I was convinced that Kibandi, for his part, wasn't keeping the score, he was just driven by the drink, high on the *mayamvumbi* by then there had been so many victims, it no longer gave me any pleasure to obey my master, he had to shout for me several times, get his other self to follow me round the whole time, threaten to kill me, though I knew he couldn't carry out that particular piece of intimidation because that would be the end of us, and so, my dear Baobab, our nighttime activities began to falter

the eyes of the local population were all on my master, who seemed to be acting on auto-pilot, we'd had difficulty pulling off our hundredth mission, I'd lost count of our failed attempts, my quills seemed to be losing their power, missing the target, as happened with the woman they call Ma Mpori, I hit her in the calf, but my quills had no effect on her at all, which should have made Kibandi sit up, now my master wanted me to carry out the mission again, but it is unthinkable, reckless, even, to attack the same person twice, I know this woman too had *something*, she was not an ordinary being, she had made this quite clear to me by asking me several times who had sent me, who was my master, only an initiate would ask that kind of question, and thinking about old Ma Mpori now, I realize that if had we doubled our level of vigilance my master would not now be rotting away in his grave, but I'll tell you this, old Mpori was something else, I am sure she'd eaten a few people in this village, and why, you may ask, am I speaking of her in the past tense when she's still alive, well, she's lost all her teeth, she leaves her door open all night long, shows her naked body by way of a curse when the young folk show her disrespect, and the young ones immediately scarper, because the sight of her naked body damns you for all eternity, she's propped up on her two rickety legs, with a hide like an old reptile, there'd been no previous history between her and my master, but even so, Kibandi believed she could tell what we got up to at night, she bothered us, she was a danger, we needed to wipe her out, it was easier said than done, even if her door was wide open on the day I went to carry out my mission, it was last month, I was alone, not even Kibandi's other self was with me, unless, unknown to me, he was hiding out somewhere, Ma Mpori was inside her hut, and when I finally got inside I couldn't see a thing, as though it was the middle of the night, I could only just make out the shape of the old woman in the corner, my quills weren't moving, but I had to go ahead, I had to carry out my mission, and it was then I heard a voice murmur, 'come on then, you old beast, you'll soon find out what Ma Mpori's made of, I'll strip naked for you', she could see me, but I couldn't see her, and she added, 'you've been doing things in this village with the one who sent you here, but you won't do that to me, you fool, you've come to the wrong place', I began to feel afraid, I wanted to go back the way I'd come, but it seemed the door behind me had closed, there was just a wall, it must have been a trick of the eye, 'who is your master, then, who sent you here, it's Kibandi the carpenter, isn't it, I know it is' she shouted at me, and when I didn't reply Ma Mpori stood up, suddenly the old hag seemed full of energy, 'tell me yourself who your master is, don't you think you've eaten enough people in this village now, what about Youla's baby, that was you too, wasn't it', then, bless my quills, I had to steel myself, she was heading straight for me, she had something in her hand, a machete, I thought, though I wasn't exactly sure, I managed to quickly cock a quill, I fired it at her, I heard her shout 'you filthy beast, what have you done to my leg, eh, just you wait till I catch you,' I looked for a way out in the pitch darkness, I aimed straight for the door, found myself outside, the old woman came out of her hut, suddenly agile on her matchstick legs, she stood there talking in front of her shack, 'evil spirits of this village, I see you at night, you bad people, you sorcerers, when you see my door left open, like it is now, it means I'm setting a trap for you, so come on back, why don't you, then you'll see me naked, right up close', I was already a way off, it was my greatest fear, my heart was pounding, if I'd had the courage I would have said to my master that we had reached the limits of our activity, that we must on no account cross the red line, but alas I said nothing, all that happened was I got told off by Kibandi, he was really horrible to me, he had forgotten my devotion, everything I had ever done for him, he called me a good for nothing, and threatened once more to kill me, and it was that day I understood his connection with his other self, my master actually pointed out his other self lying on the last mat Mama Kibandi ever wove, and said 'you see that guy lying over there, well just lately he's been getting hungrier and hungrier, it's not the moment to start bungling things, this guy needs to eat, or you'll pay the price, you don't realize that whenever he gets hungry it's me that suffers', and he told me I must make up for my failure, this time by attacking the Moundjoula family, they were a couple who'd arrived in Séképembé recently with their two children, twins, who, so he claimed, had been disrespectful to him, my master had no inkling at that point that he'd just signed his own death warrant, by giving me the mission which would turn out to be our hundredth success, sorry, make that hundred and first, since we'd be killing two birds with one stone bless my quills, how time flies, my voice is raw, night has fallen over Séképembé already, I weep and weep, I don't know why, for once my solitude is a burden to me, I feel so guilty, I did nothing to save my master, was there anything I could have done to stop those two kids who tormented him so in the few weeks before his death, I don't know, I really don't, at first I just wanted to save my skin even though I was sure that if Kibandi died I must die also, and under conditions like that, it's true what they say, better a live coward than a dead hero, well I'm not exactly overcome with grief at Kibandi's absence, nor embarrassed to have been lucky enough to survive till now, to have had you as my confidant, but I'm ashamed of all the things I've been telling you since this morning, I wouldn't want you to judge me without taking into account the fact that I was just an underling, a shadow in Kibandi's life, I never learned to disobey, it was as though I was gripped by the same anger, the same frustration, the same bitterness, the same jealousy as my master, and I don't like my present state of mind, because I'm constantly haunted by the faces of our victims, they may have vanished, but they are still here, before me, around me, watching me, pointing at me, on each face you can read the reason why we decided to finish them off, it would take me a year to explain it all, for example, young Abeba, we ate him because he had teased my master for being thin when he happened to spot him half naked by the riverside, it was unforgiveable, believe me, we ate Asalaka because he called my master a sorcerer, then desecrated Mama Kibandi's grave, it's disrespectful, the dead should be left in peace, we ate Ikonongo because he dared to defend the man who desecrated Mama Kibandi's grave, which meant he approved of it, we ate Loumouanou because she had rejected my master's advances in public at the bistro *Le Marigot*, though she was the one who first came on to Kibandi, and afterwards she claimed it was my master who had gone too far, for her it had just been a game, she said Kibandi should take a look at himself in the mirror before talking to a woman like herself, you can see, remarks like this were simply intolerable, we ate old Mabélé because he was spreading lies about my master, he said it was he who'd stolen a red cockerel from the head of the village, which wasn't even true, because it's the kids in this village who carry out that kind of theft, we had eaten Moufindiri because he was one of the ones who wanted a sorcerer to come and purify the village, rid it of all those in possession of a harmful double, who did he think he was, eh, especially since my master had no wish to end up like his father, he hadn't forgotten Tembé-Essouka, the sorcerer who was responsible for the death of Papa Kibandi, we had eaten Louvounou because he claimed to have seen a strange animal that looked like a porcupine behind my master's shack, he said things like 'in some ways it was like a porcupine, you know, and in another way, what's strange is, it wasn't like a porcupine, I mean, it was a weird animal, it looked at me like one man might look at another, and it showed me its backside before disappearing into the carpenter's workshop, I swear I didn't dream it, believe me', the guy was right but he'd made the mistake of telling the village chief about it, and he then came to talk to Kibandi, singling him out, we ate Ekonda Sakadé because he had seen my master talking to me in a thicket near Mama Kibandi's grave, and he too had gone to tell the chief of the village, we ate wise old Otchombé because he opposed Kibandi's candidature for the village council on the grounds that my master was and would remain an outsider, which offended him, when what he wanted more than anything was a chance to show the village that he was just like the rest of them, we ate the grocer, Komayayo Batobatanga because he had refused to give us credit on a storm lamp and two tins of Moroccan sardines in oil, it was unfair because the whole village bought from him on credit , we had eaten old Dikamona because of her odd comings and goings every night in front of my master's shack, hoping to catch the two of us at it, my master and I, since there was a rumour going round that there was *something* about him, and the truth is, for porcupine's sake, we just began eating people at the drop of a hat, because my master's other self had to be fed and when the creature with no mouth, no ears and no nose had had his fill, it would go and settle on the last mat Mama Kibandi ever wove, scratching and farting away, no normal creature would ever have been that hungry, and just seeing him stretched out there on the mat I could tell he was hungry because often he'd turn round, fidget for half an hour then once again lie still as a corpse

there are some victims I've forgotten completely, dear Baobab, but that's because I carried out those missions during my period of apprenticeship, they were all so similar that I may well have got them muddled while trying to fill you in on what seem to me the most important facts about my career as a double to date, leading up to last Friday's mission, the most dangerous of all

I can still see that family now, they were new in Séképembé, I can still see the two kids running around shouting, they seemed to be everywhere at once, that should have aroused my suspicions, I had wanted to warn my master, but he'd already decided, his plan was in place, he wouldn't put up with the cheek of these kids, he muttered nasty things about them, he was really just looking for an alibi, a reason to pick a fight with them, but things didn't work out like that, as it happened

my master was obsessed with thirst for *mayamvumbi*, and by his other self's inexhaustible appetite, and as a result he had ignored certain basic prohibitions usually observed by those in possession of a harmful double, for example never attack twins, but he had started acting with a casualness which took my breath away, I was the cautious one now, he was convinced that by ignoring the prohibitions he would make it to the top, as though he was aiming to beat his father's record, which is why he'd been all edgy ever since the Moundjoula family came to live in Séképembé, and it's true that around the time the Moundjoulas arrived, the father of the family made a show of his pride, dragging the children around the streets as though to show off his great good fortune as father of twins to all the villagers, ignoring those residents who claimed the two children had done all sorts of damage in their fields, Kibandi scarcely knew the family, the village chief had been pleased to introduce the newcomers to the rest of the village, he had walked down the main street, stopping at every hut saying, 'Papa Moundjoula is a sculptor, his wife is a housewife and looks after the twins, two charming children,' they lived at the far end of the village, and became each day more and more integrated, so that it soon felt as though they had always lived there

I met these two *enfants terribles* in rather dreadful circumstances, they are the kind of twins who have no distinguishing features, so that even the keenest observer would have found it impossible to tell them apart, their father and mother called them both Koté or Koty, since you only had to call one of them and they'd both turn round, but deep down Papa and Mama Moundjoula always rather enjoyed confusing everyone in the village, while in fact they did secretly have a means of telling them apart, they had decided to circumcise only one of the two children, it was said in the village that the older child was circumcised, the younger one not, and whenever Papa and Mama Moundjoula get in a muddle they just take the children's clothes off to see which of them came into the world first, I swear the two of them can scarcely be more than ten or eleven years old, they are completely inseparable, they blink, scratch, cough, fart, hurt themselves, cry or fall ill at exactly the same moment, two identical entities who sleep with their arms wrapped round each other till morning light, have the same way of sitting down, with their legs crossed, and, as though to confuse things even further, the parents dress them in identical clothing, trousers with blue braces, beige cotton shirts, they each have a head the size of a brick, kept shaved by Papa and Mama Moundjoula, they are not a pretty sight, you can imagine, with their staring eyes, they don't mix much with the other children, they go running wild through the village, they like to play near the cemetery, in a huge field of lantanas, they move all the crosses around, turn them upside down, they play hide and seek, hunt down butterflies, frighten the crows, give the sparrows a hard time with their dreaded catapults, they're uncontrollable, they always pop up where you don't expect them, the first time I came across Koty and Koté my quills were erect, by way of warning, the twins wanted to use me to play with the moment they saw me moving about in the field of lantanas, in fact I had just come from my hide-out, and was having a rest on Mama Kibandi's grave, I was about to go and have a wander about behind my master's old workshop, and perhaps read for a bit without straying far from Kibandi's hut, just in case he needed me, and the two kids heard me rustling about in the leaves, they turned round, one of them pointed to me, 'a porcupine, a porcupine, let's catch him', the other kid started to load his catapult, and bless my quills, I flung myself into an about turn, while their missiles landed a few metres away, I wondered where on earth they could have come from, these two rascals with rectangular heads, at one moment I decided they must be little ghosts whose parents, down in their graves, had given permission to go and play outside, as long as they were back before sunset, but the pair of good-for-nothings decided to follow me, I heard them brushing the lantanas aside, whooping for joy, laughing like two dwarves at a fair, one of them ordered the other to go to the right, while he stayed on the left, so they could jump out at me a few hundred metres further, they didn't realise I understand human language, and could foil their plan, I curled up in a ball and began to roll at top speed, I landed in a pile of dead bracken, in front of me I saw a thicket of thorns, I plunged into it without a backward glance, and arrived at last in a clearing overlooking the river, without thinking I plunged into the water, which is quite shallow there, I was panting desperately, I reached the opposite bank, I shook my quills, but I was trembling more with fear than cold, the village came into view, I could hear nothing behind me, I therefore concluded that the kids must have turned back, I wasn't certain they lived in Séképembé, but several days after this episode, when I saw them crossing the main street with their father, I recognise their rectangular shaped heads, and their matching clothing last Tuesday, early in the afternoon, Koty and Koté escaped from their parents again and came past my master's hut as he sat in front of his door reading an esoteric book, the twins had been popping up like this for a while now, they'd stand opposite his house, on the exact spot where my master had seen the strange flock of sheep on the day Mama Kibandi died, and the two children seemed to be spying on him, imitating the bleat of an old sheep having its throat slit, they sniggered, then vanished, this really wound my master up, he was sure the two children had been sent by their parents to annoy him, and when he finally got up to go and talk to them, tell them they owed him some respect, the kids scarpered, then came back again the next day and took up their post on the same spot, imitating the old sheep again, I could see my master was growing uneasy, asking himself questions, these two children had some message for him, they knew something about us, so that Tuesday afternoon Koty and Koté took up their position as usual opposite my master's hut, my master tried smiling at them, the two little urchins didn't smile back, 'what do you want then', Kibandi said, at last, one of the little Moundjoulas answered 'you're a bad man, that's why you don't like children' and my master, somewhat taken aback at this, answered 'you little rascals, you know nothing, why are you calling me a bad man, you'd better watch out or I'll tell your father', and the other kid added, 'you're a bad man because you eat children, we know you ate a baby, he told us when we were playing in the cemetery, and he'll tell us the same thing again tonight', my master snapped his book shut, his anger got the better of him, he jumped up, crying, 'band of vermin, birds of ill-omen, little lice, I'll teach you to respect your elders', he was about to run after the twins, when one of them shouted, '*and that baby you ate, he told us to tell you he's watching you, he's coming to see you, it's your fault he's stopped growing*', and the two brats ran off, Kibandi saw them vanish over the horizon, he decided that whatever happened, he must go and see the parents of these little creatures my master went to see the Moundjoula family that same Tuesday, in the late afternoon, the father was carving a hideous-looking mask, the mother was preparing a dish of manioc leaves with plantains, the couple were surprised to see him because he'd never set foot in their compound before, the father immediately put down his work, hastily offered their visitor a raffia chair, the mother waved him welcome from a distance, perhaps Kibandi would like to drink some palm-wine, he said no, even if it was *mwengué*, the mother brought him some cold water in a gourd and then left the two men to talk between themselves, my master tried to peer inside the house in the hope of spotting the two children, they weren't there, perhaps down in the cemetery, in the lantana field, after a few more general comments on the Moundjoulas' roof frame, which, in his opinion, was badly constructed, Kibandi explained the purpose of his visit, coming straight to the point, 'your twins have been disturbing me for the past two weeks, they came and bothered me again earlier this afternoon', Papa Moundjoula paused for a moment, then replied, 'I know, I know, they're a pair of little pests, I'll talk to them, they're always wandering about, you're not the first to complain, but you know how it is, at their age, they don't understand the consequences of their actions', then my master explained that the two kids had said he was a bad man, they didn't even say hello to him in the street, they had said things to him which he chose not to repeat out of respect for their parents, Papa Moundjoula looked at Kibandi, and you could see in his eyes, that as a father he felt sorry for him, he probably imagined the children had been teasing my master for being thin, they must have found it so strange that they hadn't tried to hide their real feelings, and just as Papa Moundjoula was asking Kibandi what it was the two children had said about him, Koty and Koté arrived with their clothes covered in dust, they threw only a cursory glance at their father and his visitor and went rushing over to their mother shouting that they were hungry, the pot was still on the fire, and the mother said 'that will teach you not to go running around the village all day long, your food isn't ready', Papa Moundjoula called them to him with an authoritative air, 'Koty, Koté, come and say you're sorry to Uncle Kibandi, right away, he's not a bad man, I don't want you being disrespectful to your elders', the two kids reluctantly came over, and the father said to the first one, 'you shake his hand, he's your uncle, all the grown-ups in this village are your uncles, you must respect Uncle Kibandi like you respect me, he has the right to spank you if you're rude again', Kibandi held out his dry, skeletal hand to Koty, or maybe Koté, who looked at it with distrust and suspicion, then held out his own, the child looked Kibandi straight in the eye, there was a kind of silence, then suddenly his face transformed, growing smoother, younger, the big, bare head was covered with soft hair, grew rounder, my master felt a kind of electric shock run through his body, he saw the head of the infant Youla in place of that of the twin who was shaking his hand 'don't look at grownups like that' Papa Moundjoula said, and as he shook the hand of the other twin my master had the same vision, again the head of the baby we'd eaten, he quickly dropped his gaze, Papa Moundjoula hadn't noticed anything, the kids apologised to my master, but were careful to add, with a touch of irony, 'see you soon Uncle Kibandi, we'll come and see you Friday', and again with irony, they chorused, 'have a good evening Uncle Kibandi' and Papa Moundjoula breathed a sigh of satisfaction at his twins' behaviour, 'you'll see, they're extraordinary kids, very likeable, once you connect with them, they'll be coming to play with you every day in your yard', but Kibandi was lost in thought, fixed on the image of baby Youla's head, he didn't dare look at the twins, he knew now that he was going to have to see to these two, they seemed to be the only people who knew about our nocturnal activities, and so he declined the Moundjoulas' offer of dinner, saying he had some urgent work to see to, which needed to be done before nightfall, and he left, without looking back, talking to himself as he went, he almost tripped over a stone, he sat drinking *mayamvumbi* all night long, I heard him cackling to himself in a way he didn't usually, repeating over and over the name of the baby we'd eaten, his laughter was a façade, I discovered for the first time that my master too could be frightened out of his wits after the Tuesday when my master went to complain to Papa Moundjoula, his life was one little mishap after another, and on the evening of that same day, around the stroke of midnight, he heard a baby crying behind his workshop, he heard children sniggering, the sound of frantic footsteps, and things diving into the river, he heard flying beasts settling on his roof, it was impossible to sleep, he lay watching and waiting till dawn, then the following morning decided that enough was enough, and for the first time, to my great surprise, he summoned me in broad daylight, I realised then he had lost it, no initiate ever summoned his harmful double in broad daylight to brief him for a mission, but I couldn't disobey him, so I left my hiding place, I had lost that spring in my step that I had back in the days when things were working out as we'd planned, this was an emergency, till now we had attacked living people, we had never confronted the shades of night, no one we had ever eaten had come back to settle with us, and when I got to Kibandi's house I pushed the door open with my paw, and stood there in the entrance, imagine my surprise, I saw a man distraught, a man who had spent the entire night drinking *mayamvumbi*, his face haggard, as though he had not slept for two or three moons, there was fear in his eyes, he told me to enter, looked at me, murmured words I couldn't catch, I said to myself we must be going to leave the village of Séképembé, and accept the fate of his family, which was to roam forever, in search of a new place to live, but instead he spoke to me of the twins, he was obsessed with them, he said the two kids were more powerful than he had realised, that we must see to them by Friday at the latest, that he did not wish me to return to the forest before this mission, which meant more to him than all the ninety-nine others before, and so I spent the day in a dark corner of his hut while he lay lifeless on his mat, the twins didn't return to disturb my master while I was there that night, but the calm was deceptive, on Friday, around the stroke of ten in the evening, while we were getting ready to make our way towards the Moundjoulas' lot, my master and I were startled by the sound of night birds scrabbling on the roof of the hut, a violent wind blew the door of his hut to bits, my master's former workshop flew apart, we were blinded by a flash of light, as though day was breaking in the middle of the night, and in the yard we saw baby Youla, the one we'd eaten, he seemed to be in fine shape, he was pointing at us, and with him were his two bodyguards, the twins Koty and Koté, they had captured my master's other self, it was painful to watch, it was as though Kibandi's other self had not even the strength of a scarecrow planted in a corn field, he was passive, like a puppet, a clown, a marionette stuffed with cotton, rags, sponge, and the two rascals were tossing him about as their fancy took them, rolling him in the dust, trying to stand him upright, my master's other self's legs would not hold, his head flopped down onto his chest and his arms dangled down by his legs, the kids were sniggering, Kibandi barked an order at me, ' go on, *throw*, throw your quills, damn you', but alas, my spikes would not move, I was petrified by what I saw, and then the twins let my master's other self fall to the ground, they came towards us, they came level with baby Youla, they looked quite different, transformed, as though they were not the same little fellows who had chased me at the cemetery, Kibandi stepped backwards, we quickly retreated into the hut, we heard them coming like a herd of a thousand cattle, the earth shuddered beneath their feet, and the walls of the hut trembled, in they came, I had curled myself up small in a corner, Kibandi had run into his bedroom, I saw him come back out with a spear in his hand, the twins and the baby doubled up laughing, pointing at his weapon, my master took up his stance and tried to throw the spear, his hands were heavy, so heavy that the weapon fell at his feet, one of the twins leapt towards him, the other seized his right foot, they pulled together, while baby Youla sniggered just outside the door, and I saw Kibandi collapse on the ground like an old tree felled with a single blow, I don't know what the little furies did to him after that because I closed my eyes I was so frightened, I heard a sort of report, like a gun firing, and yet there was no firearm in my master's hut, and the twins carried none either, I was trembling like a fool, the blinding light which had appeared when they arrived disappeared as though by magic, night fell upon us as baby Youla raised his left hand to the sky, as though he could command all nature, from my hiding place I could see his firmly planted little legs, and as he turned his burning gaze in my direction I realised he had flushed me out, that I would not be spared, his eyes bored deeper and deeper into me, he seemed to be saying that I too was finished, just like my master, who lay by the door, I began to panic, then to my surprise, the baby looked away, I thought maybe he didn't want to attack me himself, that he was going to order the twins to deal me the same punishment as my master, but no, all he did was look back at me, nod at me, asking me to flee, I couldn't believe it, I didn't hang about though, I scuttled off discreetly, I was crossing my master's bedroom when I heard a long gasp, his final breath, it was his last minute on this earth, and I went on running out into the night like a fugitive

It's getting late, dear Baobab, the moon has just disappeared, I feel my eyelids growing heavy, my limbs giving way, my sight misting over, could this be death, folding its arms about me, I can't hold out much longer, I'm slipping away, I'm tired now, oh yes, I'm very tired

how this porcupine isn't
finished yet

day has just broken, I'm surprised to find life still going on around me, the birds have come to perch on the branches of the trees, the river tumbles along, it's reassuring, all this movement, another small victory, I think I must take it as such, time seems to have flown by since yesterday, I was happy to talk to you till my eyelids began to droop, in the end you didn't once interrupt me, I still don't know what you think of this story, well, whatever, I feel better now I've got it off my chest, there may be a few things I've haven't told you, my name, for instance, which was given to me by my master, he called me Ngoumba, in our language that means porcupine, Kibandi perhaps rather liked the idea that I was not just a porcupine, an ordinary everyday porcupine, well he would wouldn't he, he was a human being, and since I didn't like this ugly sounding name, I pretended I hadn't heard him when he called me by it, but he would insist, so now you see why I didn't tell you my name right at the start

just now I was stretching out and I discovered some provisions just behind the foot of your trunk, I wonder if there isn't someone else living here, but I haven't seen a single animal go by since yesterday and logically speaking, they must belong to me now,

I daren't begin to think they might have been left here by my master's other self, I would have heard him coming like when he used to appear, he vanished too, the day the little monsters, those kids tossed him about like a marionette

I've only one regret, which is, I can't hear your voice, dear Baobab, and if you could talk like me, I'd feel less alone, but what really counts at this point is your presence, it calms my fears, and if I see danger approaching, believe me, I'll climb up into the crook of one of your branches, you'd never deliver me into the hands of death, surely, I apologise in advance for doing my business here, I'm still afraid to leave, I might do something stupid, I'd miss your protection, I don't know how long this state of alert's going to last, I know you're not wild about me defecating underneath you, though men do say excrement makes your fruits and leaves grow so in a sense I'm contributing to your eventual longevity, it's all I can offer in exchange for your hospitality

in fact, try as I might, I'm just not hungry, but I really must eat, these palm nuts don't taste like they used to though, I pass them from paw to paw, I sniff them, I try to cram a few into my mouth, they taste bitter, I don't have the strength to chew them, I know it comes from my general state of panic and fear these last few days, I must try to chill out, to relax, you can't eat when your heart's beating fast, I feel I would like to eat, just to reassure myself, and maybe so I won't die of hunger, and since last Friday I think I've lost weight, my tongue feels all mushy, my tail hangs low, my eyes are red, my limbs feel heavy and when I cough, because I've been coughing a lot just in the last few hours I feel as though I'm going to vomit up my own lungs, I can go a long time yet without eating, I don't care because my belly doesn't feel empty, and if I must die, I'd much rather die of hunger it's a sunny Monday and I feel I'd like to make some long term resolutions, take an optimistic view of the future, have no care for tomorrow, a voice inside me says I'm not going to die tomorrow, nor the day after tomorrow either, that there must be a explanation for all this, it's not up to me to go out and find it, whoever created the universe probably realises I was only the victim of the traditions of the people of this country, my survival is one in the eye for anyone thinking in future of transmitting a harmful double to their children, how much longer can I expect to live now, eh, I've no idea, dear Baobab, 'sufficient unto the day is the evil thereof' our old governor would have said, despite everything he did have some influence on my behaviour, deep down I admire him, there've been times when I've missed the old sour-face, I'd have liked to hear one of his little lectures again, one of his really brilliant ones, like the day when he spoke to us about *matter*, of the three most usual states and how they change, the *liquid state*, the *gaseous state* and the *solid state*, he could see we weren't convinced and wanted concrete examples, so tried to explain, as best he could, the meaning of *fusion, sublimation, becoming solid, becoming liquid,* or *vaporisation,* poor old guy, he was a porcupine worthy of the name, he must be dead for years now, as must the others of my generation, I'm sure

I never asked to survive, no more than I will ever ask to die, I'm content to go on breathing, see what use I can be of in the future, I've got two ideas I'd like to follow up, first I'd like to wage a merciless campaign against all the harmful doubles in this country, I know that's a big undertaking, but I'd like to hunt them down, one after the other, by way of atonement, to wipe out my share of responsibility for the misfortune suffered by this and many other villages, and second, dear Baobab, I'd simply like to go back and live in our old territory because spending so much time with men has made me nostalgic, it's a feeling you might call *territory-sickness*, men would say home-sickness, a longing for their country, I cling to my memories as the elephant clings to his tusks, distant images, vanished shades, far off noises which stop me doing something irreparable, oh yes, irreparable, I do think of that too, of taking my own life, but it's the most cowardly of all acts, and just as human beings believe their existence comes from a supreme being, I have come to believe it too, since last Friday, the reason I'm still alive, for porcupine's sake, must be because some higher will than mine has decreed it, and if so, I must have one last mission to carry out here below

I've got some other projects in mind, dear Baobab, for example, I'd like to meet a nice female, not just for some basic copulation to procreate like other animals, but for pleasure, first of all, my partner's pleasure and my own, and then, of course to make babies with, if we found we had things in common, and then, once I was a father, I would tell my offspring the story of my life, and about the ways of men, I'd warn my offspring against a calling anything like my own, and, dear Baobab, you're going to think me unreasonable, ambitious, above all, unrealistic, considering I'm 42 years old, but you know, age doesn't worry me, for porcupine's sake, I've read in the big book of God that humans used to live for hundreds and hundreds of years, their patriarch, whose name was Methuselah even lived to be 969, what I mean is, I'm not a washed-up old porcupine yet, I'd like to be the Methuselah of the animal kind, I've got some stamina yet, some life in me, what matters is to dedicate the time I have left to doing good, and only good, perhaps transform myself into a peaceful double

yes, I've still some stamina left, and I'm sure my powers are intact, aha, I see you're waving your branches in disbelief, you think I've lost all my powers, is that it, you want me to give you proof here and now, well let's have a go, I'll just get to my feet, I'll just roll up in a ball, just concentrate for a moment, and bim, bam, boom, bless my quills, did you see that, I let fly three of my quills, what's more, they came to rest a few hundred metres off, further even than when I was working for my master, what further proof do you need, I'm clearly far from finished yet

Appendix

Letter from the Stubborn Snail concerning the origin of the manuscript *Memoirs of a Porcupine*

Monsieur Stubborn Snail

Literary executor of Broken Glass

Bar owner of Credit Gone West

To Editions du Seuil

27, Rue Jacob

75006 Paris - France

Subject: Submission of manuscript *Memoirs of a Porcupine*, posthumous text by my friend Broken Glass

Madame, Monsieur,

I am writing to you in my capacity as literary executor to my lifelong friend, the late Broken Glass. I should like this letter to be published at the end of his book *Memoirs of a Porcupine*, to inform the readers of certain details regarding the origin of the text.

Last year, just after his death, I sent you, by registered post, what I believed to be his one and only manuscript, since it was I who had commissioned it, with a view to immortalising my bar, Credit gone West. You published this first text several months later under the title of *Broken Glass*, despite my having formally expressed a wish that it be called *Credit Gone West*. You appear to have decided - in the interests of the book - to take no account of this...

Be that as it may, the purpose of this letter is not to enter into a polemic on that subject. On the contrary, it gives me great pleasure to enclose this second manuscript, which one of my employees, the bartender, Mompéro, found in a thicket down by the river Tchinouka, where the body of the lamented Broken Glass was fished out. The original document - an old school folder filled with loose papers - was in such a deplorable state that great care had to be taken to put the pages together in order and number them. To this end, whenever the bar was not too busy, my two bartenders and I would sit round the table where Broken Glass usually sat. We would decipher the passages smudged with dust, rain and dew. We argued between ourselves, to avoid any temptation to ascribe to the deceased words which he had not in fact written. Our discussions, I confess, were often bitter and heated, which exasperated a number of my clients. Several of them, including the Pampers guy and Robinette, continue to deny certain scenes attributed to them in the novel *Broken Glass*. As a result, they were most displeased to hear of the existence of a second notebook, thinking, wrongly, as it happens, that *Memoirs of a Porcupine* was simply a sequel to *Broken Glass*! In fact they were worried that once again they would find themselves caricatured by the man they continue to regard as an outright traitor who stole whole sections of their lives before going to join his mother in the murky waters of the river Tchinouka

But let us return to the new manuscript!

Once the difficult task of piecing the work together was done, I personally engaged a student at the Technical Lycee of Kengué-Pauline to type up *Memoirs of a Porcupine*. She invoiced me, believe it or not, to the tune of 2000 CFA per page, that is to say, the cost of a bottle of good red wine in my bar! She justified the high cost per page of typing by saying that Broken Glass's handwriting was indecipherable, and the poor girl sometimes had to read the same line twice or three times over, all because of the author's determination to use only commas by way of punctuation.

These difficulties, dear Monsieur, dear Madame, account for the late arrival of this manuscript, and it is with great relief that I enclose it herewith, along with the original document, in order that you may, should it prove necessary, check certain of our reconstructions, particularly in the last two sections, entitled respectively 'on how last Friday became black Friday' and 'how this porcupine isn't finished yet'. These sections were the most damaged of the entire document.

Broken Glass is absent from the text, featuring neither as omnipresent narrator nor as a character in the story. Deep down he was convinced that the books we really remember are those which reinvent the world, revisit our childhood, pose questions about the origin of all things, examine our obsessions and question our beliefs. Accordingly, in this final tale entitled *Memoirs of a Porcupine* - and I sincerely hope that this time you will not change the book's title - Broken Glass was providing an allegorical version of his own last wishes. As he sees it, the world is just an approximate version of a fable which we will never understand as long as we continue to take account only of the material representation of things.

I must confess that I was quite carried away by this tale of the fortunes and misfortunes of this singular porcupine, so likeable, chatty and restless, with his deep knowledge of human nature and his way, even up to the final page, of wielding digression like a weapon, his aim being to draw a portrait of us human beings, and often, indeed, to blame us. And reading it has changed my view of animals. After all, which is really the beast, man or animal? A huge question!

I look forward to collaborating with you once again, and offer you, Madame, Monsieur, my most respectful greetings,

Stubborn Snail
Literary executor to Broken Glass
Bar owner, *Credit Gone West*